BROKEN
BY
YOU

Susan Harris

To: Jane

Thank you for your
Support, hope it is as
good as the other two

Susan Harris

Published in 2015 by FeedARead.com Publishing –
Arts Council funded

A CIP catalogue record for this title is available from
the British Library.

Acknowledgements

I never thought that I could do this and when my journey started in 2011 it was all but a dream; little did I know what would be born, the friends I would make and the places I would go.

To Kelly Joanne Grainger, our workshop together in my car paid off and the title of this book is dedicated to you.

To Carla Hitchen, always spreading the word and promoting my books.

To all my friends that sadly lost their jobs, you have gone onto bigger and better things and I am glad that I had several years knowing you all. To all my new friends in the North East, I'm glad I have had the chance to meet you.

To Peter, I have worked you harder than most but thank you as always for you continued contribution, input and hard work on my books.

And finally to Natalie Jenns, you gave me some great feedback and I hope you like what I did in return.

You asked and I listened and "The Trilogy" is now complete.

What else can I say, people, except, "Thank you, from the bottom of my heart"?

BROKEN
BY
YOU

Susan Harris

Titles by Susan Harris

I Promise You

Because Of You

You can visit the author's website at:
www.susanharrisbooks.co.uk

Chapter One

Isobelle gave nothing away as she rolled Jack's lifeless body away from Autum and wrapped herself around him, cuddling him. Autum couldn't move or speak and just watched Isobelle as she started to rock – back and forth, back and forth – holding Jack close to her body...

I slowly lifted myself up from the ground, not concerned about the amount of blood on my clothes, and looked at Isobelle. And as she looked back at me, I saw those same evil eyes and streaks of mascara running down from them. It felt like I could even see all the hate-filled thoughts filling her mind at that moment. I tried to speak but no words would leave my mouth and as it seemed that was how she wanted it, I was only happy to oblige. Instead, I headed towards my parents, giving Isobelle time with Jack in private. As I turned around one last time, she was wiping the blood from his brow as she planted kisses there. I watched how she curled away the strands of his dark brown hair that fell around his face and gently tucked them behind his ear. I saw how her face lit up and the way she smiled at him as she began to talk to him. I turned back around to face my parents and my tears started to fall again, heavier than before. *Why, Jack? Why?* I killed Jack… Not deliberately but I did. Jason would never believe I had not meant to do it – and why would he? *His only son is dead, because of me.* I wrapped my arms around myself, feeling cold, helpless and alone. I bent down towards my mother who took me in her arms, where I felt warm, protected and safe.

"Shush," she said as she wiped the tears from my cheeks.

"You know I didn't mean to hurt him, don't you, Mum? But he…"

"Don't do this to yourself, Autum. We were all there. We saw what he was going to do. Any one of us would have done the same." She held me tighter.

I took a look over my mum's shoulder at Jack and my stomach clenched; he looked so young, so at peace and so free. A lump blocked my throat. *I close my eyes, remembering the good times, when Jack was Jack and we both didn't have a care in the world…* Isobelle and I met him at a nightclub… He wrote his number on a piece of tissue paper and slipped it into my hand as he left with his friends. *I can still feel the buzz of excitement it gave me when I opened my hand and saw his number and his initial, "J".* I held off for two whole days, debating what I should do, and then I asked Isobelle for advice.

"Call him, silly!" was her response. And so I did.

We had been dating for three months before I found out he was running his own company. I could understand why: he probably didn't want some gold-digger who was in love with his money rather than in love with him. We never spoke about past relationships and I believe we always got on so well because we liked the same things: movies, holidays, dining out and time with our friends and because we never crowded each other but both had our own space. It worked for nearly three years. *I think back to when he asked me to meet him at work for the first time.* I went into the huge glass reception and the lady behind the desk asked if I had come for a meeting. I smiled and told her that I was meeting a friend who worked there – a Mr Cartwright. She smiled and told me to take a seat and that she would let Mr Cartwright know that I was there. *It makes me smile, remembering how formal his name sounded.* I still only thought he was a member of staff and then the receptionist told me that his assistant would come down to meet me. At first, I wondered whether there was another Mr Cartwright and if there had been a mix-up. I was escorted to the seventh floor through a very busy office, then on down a long corridor until the assistant finally stopped outside a large office and told me that I would be OK to go in. I looked at her and said,

"I think there must be some mistake; I was looking for a 'Jack' Cartwright?" She looked back at me, puzzled.

"Yes. This is his office." She opened the door and ushered me in.

I start to laugh inwardly as I remember Jack's expression as he saw my face, open-mouthed, turning to get the full view of the office. My mind had gone blank and I only came out of my trance when I felt Jack in front of me, giving me a kiss to snap me out of my shock. He had sat me down and talked about his business, his father and his future plans. *My eyes blink open, startling me. His body is still lying there. I can feel my mother's warmth around me. I close my eyes again. I remember being in his office months later.* Jack was about to take a call from his father, Jason: it would be our first joint encounter with his father. I saw his face come through on the video-conference screen and it was startling how much the two men looked alike. Jason's voice was different though: always in control, always the firmest, the most direct and the sharpest. He was a businessman, alright, and despite their looks, sometimes you could nearly forget they were father and son. Jason always went straight to business-talk with his son, then struggled to chat afterwards. But when Jack introduced me as his girlfriend, Jason started to soften a little bit. Jack loved when I was there, as he knew his father loved speaking to me, sometimes more than to Jack. He used to tell me that his father was becoming soft when it came to me and I used to laugh it off.

I think of all the times we spent together and all the times we made love and I wonder what went wrong? How did it end up like this? They say things happen for a reason and maybe they do, but this: no one would want this to happen, surely? He wasn't always bad, so are my actions to blame for all of this? I hope not. I blink back to reality again, knowing that I need to go to Isobelle and, even more, that I need to see Jack. I tap my mum on the shoulder so she can let me go.

"I need to speak to her, mum." She looked at me and opened her mouth to speak, the words at the tip of her tongue. But instead, she turned it into a smile and nodded, letting me go. I walked the short distance to where Isobelle was sitting and bent down for eye-contact.

"Isobelle, look at me." She continued to rock, her chin resting on Jack's forehead, so I placed my hand on her shoulder. She stopped rocking abruptly, startling me. I quickly withdrew my hand, as she slowly looked up. A scene from a horror film filled my mind but I shrugged it off.

"You're not taking him; he loved me," she whispered, her hold on Jack getting tighter.

"I know he loved you, Isobelle. He…" But she cut me off.

"If he loved me, then why did he say all those things? I tried everything to make him love me. Everything." She was starting to shout. "But it was never enough. He told me he loved me and I was so happy. I thought we had turned a corner but then YOU spoiled it for me. I was always second best, no matter how hard I tried. What did you have that I didn't?" She stared straight at me.

I couldn't answer, as no matter what I wanted to say, this was not the right place to say it. We were all frail and on edge and even I knew that Isobelle was not in the right frame of mind to understand.

"You always got what you wanted, always thought you were better than be. But remember in the end he came to me. He left YOU for ME." She literally spat the last few words at me.

I wanted to stay so much and remind her of how this sorry tale had begun: what they had both done to me. But she knew all that already and I wasn't going back there. I wanted to express my anger, in more ways than one, about how they had both let me down but for now, I was happy for Isobelle to shift all the blame and anger and whatever else was going through her mind on to me if it made her feel any better. *We all need to be there for each other today; whether we like it or not, we all need to be together.* And with that thought, I edged closer to her and slowly put my arms around her. She stiffened at first. I was holding my breath, my heart beating erratically, before she finally relaxed and put her head on my shoulder, still holding Jack tight to her body.

"I have nothing because of you," she whispered in my ear. "You've taken the only thing that mattered away from me and I'll never forgive you, Autum. Never."

The last words felt like a threat and I knew that she would not hold anything back. But I did have to remind her of one important thing.

"He was going to kill me," I whispered.

"Yes, he was. He was going to kill YOU, no one else." She lifted her head off my shoulder and gave me an evil smile. I pulled my arms away, feeling goose bumps forming on my arms and a chill running down my spine as she continued.

"All this." She nodded her head towards my parents and around the building. "This was to get you here. He would never hurt me or your parents. It was all a front. The only person that should be dead right now is you, not Jack... not Jack..." Her words tapered off and she started to cry. I had heard no remorse in her words, no "I'm-only-saying-this-because-I'm-upset". She wanted me dead.

"So why did you step in front of me to block him when he came at me? You could have got what you wanted."

"Because I was a fool, a fool who thought that Jack would be proud of me, a fool for making you survive instead of him and a fool to think we could ever be friends."

Yes, it was all coming out. I moved away from Isobelle. She was too angry and I was too emotional. My insides had started to go all funny and I was starting to get the shakes.

"You're a murderer, Autum. Live with that." A hysterical laugh left her mouth.

I stopped in my tracks and took in those vicious words. *A murderer...* I went to a corner and threw up and then ran from the building, feeling suffocated, stifled and desperate for air. My phone popped into my head and I ran towards my car, hoping that I still had battery life. I found my phone under the seat where it had fallen – I still had ten percent battery. I was so grateful to the Lord that I thanked him as I kissed my phone. I called for two ambulances and explained that there had been a fatality and that there were several injured parties. I gave them Jack's full name and explained briefly what had happened. I tried as best as I could to describe my location but asked if they could track my phone, if possible, as I didn't really have a clue where I was. They told me to describe roughly how far we had travelled once we left the road and asked if there were any markings on the building. I could just make out large letters on the building's side but most of them had disappeared, rusted away over the years. I could only make out the words "steel industries". I told them to hurry and to get to us as fast

15

as they could before I hung up. My heart was racing. I think hearing someone else's voice had got the adrenaline pumping. I needed to go back inside to let the others know that the ambulances were on their way.

It felt like a lifetime in that derelict building after I returned but, eventually, I heard the noise of sirens blaring. The thought that Isobelle would be more than happy to hand me over to the police as a murderer... *God*... that played so heavily on my mind. Everyone stopped and listened, focusing on the noise. I looked at Isobelle and she just smiled. *God knows what's going on in that head of hers.*

I left my mother still reassuring my dad that everything would be OK. When Jack had swung that pipe at him, it had caught him right in the chest, possibly breaking some ribs. He was in so much pain.

I made my way outside so that the ambulance crews would know where we were. I didn't know whether my call had created this response or whether Rebecca had managed to call as well but there were four police cars and two ambulances approaching at top speed. As I waved them over, it really looked like a scene from those American Crime Investigation shows. When the police cars pulled up, I was relieved to see Rebecca running over to me. She stopped abruptly and I wondered what was wrong. But then I followed her eyes and realised that she was focusing on the blood on my clothes, something I had forgotten about.

"Jesus, Autum, you're covered in blood." She started to blabber about the phone call that she had received from me, explaining how, as soon as my voice had completely faded, she had got off the phone and rung the police. She was speaking so quickly, as if she was going to forget what she needed to say so had to say it all in one breath. She stretched out her arms towards me but... *I can't take it, I can't embrace her and I don't know why. That's a lie. I do. I don't want to be held, I don't deserve all this affection. I am a murderer and murderers don't deserve any sympathy.* I backed away from her and she started to call my name. Policemen were heading in my direction and I started to hyperventilate. *They're coming to get me, take me away. They know I killed him.* More and more things started to enter my head. I was losing it, big-time. Keep calm, I told myself, and breathe. But before I could get the chance to work on my breathing, I saw someone else coming out of a police car: *Jason.* I felt my legs giving out below me, as I looked for Rebecca.

"Autum!" Rebecca caught me before I fell; I heard her screaming for an ambulance as I opened my eyes.

"I'm fine," I said in a hypnotised voice. "I can't speak to him, Rebecca."

"Who? The police?"

"Jason. He won't understand. He will blame me for everything."

"Autum, you're scaring me. Why would he blame you? What have you done?" Her eyes took in the blood on my clothes again.

"Is that your blood?" she whispered, holding me at arm's length.

I could see that she was thinking hard. I knew she must have one hundred and ten questions that she was dying to ask but she only rubbed her forehead and sighed.

"No, it's… it was… it's Jack's." I stopped speaking as police officers and medics surrounded me.

I pointed to the building and informed them that there were several casualties and a fatality. I told them to leave me and see to them first and that I would be OK. I inwardly laughed to myself. *OK? I will never be OK again.* I heard Rebecca repeat the word "fatality" and I nodded.

Jason was heading my way. I wondered if they had informed him that it was his son who had died. The look in his eyes and the blankness behind them confirmed he knew. I stared at him and he stopped. *Maybe he can see the turmoil in my eyes, sense the pain and the hurt.* I struggled to form words as he started to move closer again, my eyes never leaving his. He walked straight past me.

"Jack's dead," I hear Rebecca say. I can see medics leaving the building with a body bag. Jason stops abruptly. Isobelle is among the medics, scarcely able to stand, sobbing uncontrollably. Jason's cry echoes around me, startling me. I watch his pace quicken towards the medics. He says something to them and then they stop to unzip the bag. I watch intently how he strokes his son's face then bends down to kiss it over and over. A medic lays a hand on his shoulder, letting him know that they need to go. The bag is zipped up again and they head towards the ambulance. As they approach me, I try and reach out to Jason to say that I'm sorry but Isobelle blocks me and stops.

"You killed him," is all she says. I see Jason look up at me as they climb into the ambulance.

My father is next out of the building, my mother holding his hand. He raises his head towards me and I give a pathetic smile to reassure him. There is no room for me in the ambulance, so I have to ride in the police car with Rebecca. Seeing the bars in front of me makes me think about what lies ahead of me, as we head towards the hospital. The journey is long and all I can hear are the sirens going through my head. I curl up into a ball, not saying a word and trying to drown out the noise, whilst leaning my head against the window. I'm glad that Rebecca does not push me for any more answers. She just leaves me to deal with this in my own way. I can feel her stroking the back of my hair, letting me know she is still there. I close my eyes and start to dream.

Chapter Two

Jack has still taken me but he has taken me to a different location, a penthouse suite on the forty-second floor, with magnificent views overlooking the city. It's night and the lights below us are spectacular. He guides me outside on to the balcony, the brisk night air catching my breath and a chill hitting my flesh.

"This is for you, Autum," he says, "A romantic view of the city for the woman I love." He wraps his arms tightly around me.

"Why bring me here?" I ask him, though not wanting to ruin the moment.

"Because, for every beginning, there is an end and for every life, there is death." Jack talks as if in poetry.

I feel scared. Who or what is ending?

"What do you mean?" I ask. He lets go of my waist and walks around me.

"What better way to show you how much I love you than to do this?"

He slowly walks over to the edge of the balcony.

"What the hell are you doing, Jack?" He climbs on to the ledge and turns to face me.

"I can never have you but I want to always remember this moment we both shared." And with that, he tips backwards and I scream out his name.

I was jolted awake by the police car swerving to the right. Rebecca was staring at me as if I had lost it.

"What?" I said, confused and a little disorientated.

"You screamed out… Jack's name. You gave us a fright."

I didn't say another word, just continued to stare out of the window, afraid to close my eyes again.

We arrived at the hospital and I stayed in the car until Jack's body had been removed from the ambulance and Isobelle and Jason had exited. Once I saw my parents, I then came out of the car with Rebecca and was ushered into a cubicle next to my father. I was starting to shake and could feel my skin getting clammy. I looked up at the doctor as he forced me to lie down. I cannot remember what was said after that, just felt myself slipping under, compliments of the injection I was given, blissfully unaware of what events were happening around me.

Isobelle refused to leave Jack until she was forced to, even though she knew he had gone. She consoled Jason as he sat in the waiting room, a man who had thought little of her before today. Did he want her attention? She couldn't say: he was grieving and she was there.

"I need you to tell me what happened."
Isobelle's arms were wrapped around him and his head was buried but as he spoke, he gave her a warning glance.

"Do you really want to know now? Why not wait…?" Jason cut her off.

"I said, 'Now.' Or I'll find Autum myself and find out how the hell my son ended up dead." Jason's voice was laced with anger.

"You may not like what I have to say," Isobelle replied.

"I'll be the judge of that. Now, begin."

Isobelle started to talk, letting go of Jason and standing up in the corner of the room, reliving the events of the day.

"Jack had been having a few rough nights lately, waking up in a sweat, muttering *her* name and talking in his sleep, I put it down to the events of the crash and thought that he just needed time to get over it. Then, last night, he nearly strangled me in his sleep, saying that Autum would pay over and over again until I had to shout at him to wake up. I knew it wasn't me he wanted to strangle but that bitch." Jason looked up at Isobelle, catching her gaze, before she turned away and continued. "Once he got up, he was… well, in a strange mood. He didn't say a word about what had happened. He just kept pacing up and down, mumbling under his breath, with his fists clenched. I didn't know what to do. Then he just got dressed and stormed out of the apartment."

"What time was this?" Jason asked.

"It was around five in the morning."

23

"And you never thought to ring me? Maybe if you had, my son would still be alive." Jason stood up and walked towards Isobelle.

"You're not putting the fucking blame on me, Jason, no fucking way." She stood her ground, confronting him. "Your son needed… help." She hated the fact of what she had just said but she knew it needed to be said. "Your son was so obsessed with that bitch that he was living in his own world. I thought we had turned a corner. We were happy, truly happy, for a short time. Where were you in all of this?"

Jason took a step closer to Isobelle, his face mere inches from hers.

"I loved my son." His fist clenched and he looked away, as if remembering.

"You were never there, Jason. All that money and you waited five years to visit. Some father you were…" Before she could take another breath, Jason lashed out and slapped her hard across the face. She cried out, clutching her cheek with both hands.

"I didn't mean to say that. I'm sorry." She continued to cry. Jason turned his back on her, the truth of how right Isobelle was burning in his chest as he sat back down.

"Continue," was all he said, trying to control his breathing.

In between sobs, Isobelle continued.

"He came back to the apartment around seven as I started to get ready for work. He looked… worse than when he had left. I was scared to even talk to him. Then he came up to me and told me to hurry up and that he would drive me into work. I was afraid to say 'No' so I did what he asked and we left the house around eight. I tried to break the ice and asked him if he was going for

24

his check-up at the hospital later on and he told me that he was. It was only when he started taking a different route that I knew something was wrong."

"Go on," said Jason, not giving Isobelle time to recover.

"I told him that this was not the route into work and his only reply was, 'I know.' I asked him where he was taking me and he said that he was taking me for a drivè and that I would not be going to work today. I pulled out my phone and he asked me what I was doing and I said that I could just not turn up at work and that I would need to tell them I needed the day off for personal reasons. He nodded and I made the call but soon afterwards he asked for my phone and took it away from me. It was nearly nine when he pulled into a dirt road and stopped the car.

"'Why are we here?' I remember asking him.

"'I have to do this, Isobelle. I'm sorry' was Jack's reply.

"'What do you mean you "have to do this"? Are you going to hurt me?' I said in a panicked voice.

"'Not unless you force me to. This is the only way I can get her here.' And with that, he told me to get out of the car and open the gate. Once through, I got back in and we drove until we reached a derelict building. I looked across at Jack but he gave nothing away. Once the car stopped, he told me to get out and that's when he pulled out the masking tape and I panicked and started to run."

"What happened next?" Jason was starting to sit upright now.

Isobelle paused for a moment, wrapping her arms around her waist.

"He caught me, even though I kept fighting him up until he pinned me to the floor and tied me up. As he took me into the building, he just kept telling me that it would be OK and that he wouldn't harm me. By that time I was a total wreck and just stopped fighting. We ended up on the third floor and it felt like he knew his way around the building. He didn't hesitate or stop to look around; he just headed straight on. Then he tied me up. And then he fed me. Can you believe that? He fed me and then he left me in that goddamn building. The only reason he came back was because I was screaming my head off, so he got the tape and put it across my mouth.

"I must have dosed off but I was woken by what sounded like people arguing. I kept quiet as I thought they might be tramps or drug users. I was praying that they had not seen us both come in and then only one of us leave. But the noises were getting louder and louder. Then I saw a man being thrown into the room and land just in front of me with a hysterical woman shortly afterwards. They both looked up and it was only then that I realised that he had somehow got Autum's parents there as well.

"'Isobelle,' was all they managed to say before Jack entered and they turned and looked at him. He was laughing; somehow he found this whole ordeal funny. He tied them up back-to-back, taped their mouths shut, then left. He even joked about keeping his appointment at the hospital. The next thing I remember is Autum being thrown into the room and all hell breaking loose. When she spotted her parents, she just charged at Jack like a madwoman. Then she tried several times to untie her father but Jack grabbed her and told her to say her goodbyes. When he went to take her away, she held on to a bollard and wouldn't let go. Jack tried desperately to get hold of her and take her out of the room but she managed to get away and then she picked up a pole and hit him with it.

"We thought he was dead. She kept screaming that she had killed him and said, 'Sorry,' to me. Then as she untied us all and we started to leave the building…"

"Wait, you were going to leave my son?" Jason got up again and headed towards Isobelle.

"No, no, it was not like that." Panic rose in her voice and she held out a hand to protect herself.

"We were going back to the car to call an ambulance but as we left the room, we heard a noise and when we turned around, Jack was running at us with the pole. He was going to kill us all, Jason, you need to remember that. He knocked Autum's father clear out of the way and then headed straight for Autum. She froze, couldn't move, so I stepped in front of her. Why? I don't know. Maybe deep down I thought that if he did hurt me then she would realise the sacrifice I was willing to make for her. But she pushed me out the way and when I fell, I caught hold of Jack's leg and he fell, dragging Autum down with him. He died next to her."

Isobelle turned to face Jason, whose head was still buried. He kept quiet and after a while he walked away and started to pace, putting Isobelle on edge. He looked up at her, his breathing quite heavy. The heat of his stare burned into her flesh.

"Something just doesn't feel right. Have you told me everything?"

"Of course I have! Why would I leave anything out?" But she knew that she had. Why the hell would she admit that Jack died loving that bitch and not her?

27

But she also remembered him saying how much he loved his father… She looked up to speak but Jason was gone.

Autum was taken to a ward, still suffering from shock. She had lost all sense of time and when her eyes opened, it was dark. She curled up in the bed, pulled the covers higher up her body and closed her eyes again but all she could see was Jack's face in those last moments, then Jack's face when he had charged at her, then Jack's face when they were together: constant flashes of images being played over and over again in her head. She could feel herself tossing and turning and then she jumped up and screamed. Jason stood in front of the bed.

She noticed how puffy his eyes were and knew he was a broken man.

"Jason, he was going to kill me," was all Autum could quietly say.

Jason sat on the bed as she stared intently at him, unsure of what he would do to her.

"I only meant to slow him down. He had kidnapped me, my parents and Isobelle. He had told me to say my goodbyes. I was just trying to escape. I'm so sorry, Jason. I don't know what else to say." Jason held her gaze.

"Did he say anything?"

"He told me… that he still loved me and that he could not love anybody else… I asked him what had gone wrong and we talked for a while but most of all he wanted me to tell you something." Jason's eyes widened. "He wanted me to tell you how much he loved you and that he was sorry."

Jason broke down and cried.

Chapter Three

Frank had been making steady progress. He was happy that the doctors had given him the all-clear and that they only wanted to monitor him for another week. He was even happier when Autum came to see him although he knew she felt guilty at the circumstances of why he was in hospital. He had survived, however, and that was all that mattered. The police had wanted to talk to him but Frank was in no hurry to relive the horror of what had happened. He knew that they would be back soon though and that he had to prepare himself to try and remember. The truth of the matter was that he had only remembered bits, small flashbacks, since he woke up. The doctor said that this was normal and due to the trauma Frank had suffered. In time, his memories would return – how long this would take, he did not know.

His doctor had given him advice about his recuperation and told him that he would need to have physiotherapy, which Frank was happy to do without question.

His parents had booked to come back over which he felt bad about, considering that they had not long returned home. Right then, he was just longing to see his wife again. He pressed the buzzer to get some attention and asked if it was possible to get access to his belongings so that he could ring his wife.

Autum's phone rang and it took a few seconds for it to register. When she finally answered, it was Frank's sexy voice that greeted her.

"Autum, is everything OK? I've missed your visits." Frank's voice was calm and soothing.

"Don't worry about me, Frank. Nothing seems to ever work out right for me. Nothing!" Autum started to cry.

"What's happened? You were fine at lunchtime."

"Jack's dead," was all Autum said.

"What do you mean 'dead'? Where are you?"

"We're in a local hospital…"

"What do you mean 'we'? Who are you with?"

"My parents are here, along with Jason and Isobelle. God, Frank, it's all a mess."

"I'm coming to get you. Tell me where you are."

"No, Frank, you're still recovering. I'll be fine; just need some rest. I think they will keep me in overnight then I will visit you in the morning. Please, Frank? I just can't worry about you as well."

"I understand."

Frank's voice had risen in volume but now returned to his normal calm and soothing tone and Autum felt a bit more relaxed.

"Frank, are you still there?" Autum could only hear his breathing.

"Are you hurt?" Frank knew that Autum would not let him worry. Even if she was hurt, he knew that she would probably not admit it.

"Just need some rest. I'm very tired and the doctor thinks I'm suffering from shock but I just need some sleep."

"You promise to contact me tomorrow?"

"Promise. I love you, Frank."

"I love you too. You know that. Always." And with that, a worried Frank hung up the phone and called Rebecca.

Rebecca's phone rang and she could see it was Frank on the phone. She was still waiting to see Autum and wondered if Frank had found out what had happened. She was unsure of what to do but knew that he would know if she was either lying or hiding the truth from him so she just answered the phone and hoped she could deal with whatever he had to say.

"Hello, Frank," Rebecca said cautiously.

"I have just spoken to Autum and she said that Jack is dead. Is that true?"

"Jack is dead. That is true." And with that, Rebecca started to tell Frank as much of what had happened as she could recall. She could hear Frank sighing every now and then and kept pausing to make sure he was OK. When she had finally finished, Frank spoke.

"I'm on my way." He ended the call.

"Shit! Shit…" was all Rebecca could say as panic set in. She knew Autum would be pissed if he did turn up and she wanted to warn her. She still did not know exactly where Autum was though. Maybe if she rang her on her mobile she would answer but that felt like a chicken's way out. Luckily, she met a doctor who was able to tell her where Autum's room was. She knocked gently before entering. Rebecca found her sleeping, so sat down by the bed and held her hand. Autum started to stir and turned to face her.

"Hi," said Autum, sleepily.

"Autum, I need to say something, quickly." Time was not on Rebecca's side.

Autum sat up in bed and wiped her tired eyes. "Has something happened?"

"You could say that. Frank rang me not long ago and wanted to know what happened."

"What did you tell him, Rebecca?"

"Sorry, Autum, Frank can be quite demanding and I was scared to lie to him."

"Oh, Jesus, he's on his way, isn't he?" Rebecca's silence told her he was.

"I couldn't stop him, Autum. He asked me what I knew and I told him and before I knew it, he said that he was on his way over. I'm sorry." Rebecca started to panic but Autum just held her hand.

"It's OK, Rebecca, I know Frank can be stubborn." Autum sat waiting for her stubborn husband to arrive and fifteen minutes later he walked through the doors or rather, he was wheeled in, accompanied by a nurse.

"What happened to me seeing you tomorrow?" said Autum, casting her eye over his sexy stubble, his rugged hair and those kissable lips.

"Hi, Frank, you're looking well," said Rebecca, heading out through the door. Frank gave the nurse a

34

nod and the nurse said she would be back in five minutes.

When everyone had left, Frank tried slowly to get up, obviously forgetting or stubbornly refusing to acknowledge that he had not long ago woken up from a coma. He stumbled back into the wheelchair. Autum shot out of bed to help him settle but Frank's arms were already wrapping themselves around his wife's waist and guiding her down on to his lap.

"There was no need for you to come, Frank, I was fine. You need to rest and…" Frank's lips had stopped any more words coming out. His hands started to loosen their grip but his kiss felt just as loving as always. This was a lovely gesture, the best she could have wished for after the events that she had been through.

"Autum, are you really alright?" Frank broke off the kiss to look up at his wife.

Autum lifted herself off her husband. He was weak but was too proud to admit it. He could hardly support his own weight, never mind his wife's as well. She did not want to talk about what had happened, so she changed the subject.

"The doctors said that I should be able to take you home in a week. I have given Rosetta some instructions to prepare for your homecoming and for your parents' return. They were so happy when I phoned them to tell them the good news."

"How have they been?" Frank's voice was shaky and weak.

"They have been great. They stayed on for such a long time with my parents after I lost our bab…" Autum paused.

"You lost our… baby? When? How? Talk to me, Autum." Frank's voice could not have been more pleading.

Autum knelt down beside Frank and started to speak, going over what had happened, from the kidnapping by Jason to the time of the accident. She told him that both his parents and hers knew about the baby and she told him that she needed to grieve.

"I knew I should have taken you to A&E. If I had, then…"

"Stop it, Frank, there is no one to blame here. I had no idea, that's all. I am lucky – there was no damage, so trying again shouldn't be a problem. My only concern now is to get you home and get you back to your full strength."

Before Frank could add any more to the conversation, the nurse came back in.

"It's time to get you back, Mr Howard," said the nurse, as she wrapped her hands around the handles of the wheelchair and released the brakes.

Autum got up and kissed Frank quickly.

"I'll pop in to see you tomorrow after they let me go. They just want to observe me, that's all." Autum gave him a reassuring smile.

"Love you, Frank."

"Love you too," he said, as the nurse wheeled him out of the door.

Isobelle had left the hospital, upset that Jason had barely comforted her in her grief. She was hurting, vulnerable and truly alone. She knew Jason did not approve of her and Jack's relationship but he must have known how much she was in love with his son. And it had nothing to do with his money. She was always going to have to prove herself. She had tried to do so for Jack's love and now she would have to do so for Jason's acceptance. She was always going to be the outsider but she knew she could survive, prove to all of them how wrong they had been to write her off. She wandered around for hours, clearing her head and thinking about how much she was missing Jack. She felt an emptiness filling her up. She took in a deep breath of fresh air. She needed to speak to Jason, as she wanted to play an active part in organising the funeral arrangements. That thought nearly made her sick. She decided that she needed to go back to the hospital and find Jason. She wanted him on *her side*. Together they could bring down Autum and Frank. Together they could do more damage than either of them could alone. And Jason had already done so much by himself. He had even kidnapped Autum. Yes, Isobelle needed him and she was going to do whatever was needed and play whatever part to get Jason on her side. The more she tried to put Jack's death to the back of her mind, the more she realised she wanted to avenge his death. Gone was the rational knowledge that it had been an accident; it was all about who was going to pay. That was the only way she could truly move on. She found herself breaking into a little jog as she headed back through the hospital door.

Jason was at the drinks machine as Isobelle headed towards him.

"Jason?" Isobelle's voice was soft and seductive as she placed a hand on his shoulder. Jason slowly turned and she could see how puffy his eyes had been: a man so proud that even in public he was still trying to put on his hard face. Isobelle needed to seize this opportunity. She only had a split second to gain his trust so she started to sob uncontrollably, wrapping her arms around him until she felt his arms as he hugged her in response. Her mouth formed a smile behind his back.

"I'm sorry, Jason, I truly am. I miss him so much and I feel so alone. I have no one else I can turn to." Isobelle cried some more.

"Shush, I miss him too. I just wish I had told him more often how much he meant to me. I wish I had spent more time with him, I just wish..." Jason trailed off as he found himself stroking Isobelle's back. They stayed in that embrace until Jason saw Frank being wheeled past them towards the hospital exit. He released Isobelle with a slight shove and ran towards him.

"Frank!" Jason raised his hand as he headed towards him. The nurse had come to a standstill and turned the wheelchair to face him. Each man looked the other up and down.

"Jason." Frank tried to get up but both the nurse and Jason touched him on the shoulder, a gesture for him to remain where he was. That touched a nerve; Frank was mad with himself that he was not strong enough to greet Jason properly, man-to-man.

"My condolences, Jason. I am truly sorry for your loss."

"Thank you, Frank, it means a lot," said Jason, knowing Frank's words were genuine. No matter what had gone on, Frank was a true gentleman.

"When did you, err...?" said Jason, feeling his cheeks heat a little with embarrassment.

"Woke up this morning, if that's what you were going to say. Hence the wheelchair. Can't use my legs properly at the moment; they feel like mush," said Frank, trying to laugh things off.

"I'm sorry for what my son put you through. In fact, I'm sorry for everything I put you both through. I really messed up big-time, eh?"

"Jason, we have both suffered," said Frank, pointing to himself in the wheelchair. "No one could have predicted these events, no one. I knew Jack loved Autum. Tried to understand what was going on but he was so unreadable." Frank started to rub his temple and the nurse stepped in.

"Mr Howard, I need to get you back." And without any further word, she started to wheel Frank out through the door. Jason accompanied him, trying to keep up the conversation with small talk. Just before Frank was lifted into the ambulance, he turned his chair to Jason.

"Deep down, she still loved him. I knew that. That's why most things he did to her she never reported, despite the risk to her own safety. She still wanted to let him off, thought that he would realise how lucky he had been that she hadn't pressed charges. She would not have defended herself if she was not in fear for her life and her family. You know that, don't you?"

Jason watched Frank being helped into the ambulance as a lump formed in his throat. The truth hurt. He knew Autum had only done what she did out of fear. He had seen how she was with him after *he* kidnapped her. She had forgiven him and helped him talk to his son. He was so glad that she had done that. He could not hate her. He could only thank her for those precious moments in that house with his son. He waved Frank goodbye, knowing he needed to decide if his son would come back to California or be buried here. Who would look after Jack's grave when Jason was away? He did not know.

Isobelle watched Jason and Frank talking from afar. They looked like they were best buddies and that was not the plan she had in mind. How the hell could she turn Jason into Frank's enemy? Her attempt to get close to him had seemed like it was working until he saw Frank. She was getting tired and decided to return to the apartment she had shared with Jack. As she unlocked the door, she started to cry. She could still smell his aftershave in the rooms. It felt so quiet, so empty, and she felt so alone. There was no one to comfort her, no one to tell her things would get better, *no one*. She thought about everything she had now lost and about everything Autum still had and she felt angry. She needed to sleep, to think and to work out what she was going to do.

She knew Jack had not been an angel but he had been her devil and no one else's. How could Jack have betrayed her with his last breath, in the worse possible way? Yet again, Autum had it all. As she paced up and down, she came across his favourite top and breathed him in. She closed her eyes and pictured them making love on the sofa: the things they had done to each other there, all the places his hands, mouth and tongue had been, the orgasms they had given each other, over and over again. She opened her eyes and looked at the floor, picturing Jack, a pillow under his head, lying naked, her hot lips around his cock sucking and licking, teasing then releasing so he did not come too soon, then straddling him as he sucked, bit and squeezed her nipples, holding her in place with his hands gripped firmly around her waist, lifting his hips for deeper, harder penetration. *God, it was so good.* The countless times he had taken her from behind, slightly gripping her hair but never hurting her... And the bedroom, oh God, the things that they did in the bedroom brought tears and smiles to her face. Isobelle walked to the bedroom that was now hers alone and looked in. Only hours before, they had been in bed and he had fucked her with his tongue, fingers and cock and then sucked her dry. She could still feel her clit, slightly throbbing and swollen, and she knew she would not feel his touch, his hands or his lips all over her body again. She silently wept.

I will get my vengeance, Jack. I promise you that. This will be my gift to prove my love for you.

Isobelle needed to rest. She slept with Jack's top under her chin. As she drifted off, she began to plan what she was going to do to avenge Jack's death – his murder. Because in her mind, Autum had murdered Jack. To spite her! She smiled in her sleep and imagined how she was going to make Autum beg for her life.

Chapter Four

Frank arrived back at the hospital and was helped on to the bed. Even though he would have preferred to stay in his chair, he reluctantly relaxed and felt better for it. *She was pregnant…* That's all he had thought about on the way back from his visit to Autum. He caught himself smiling at the thought of her carrying his child before the truth of her loss hit him again. *Yet another thing she's had to deal with by herself.* His mood began to darken and he was glad when a knock at the door jolted him from his thoughts and Rosetta walked into the room. A smile lit up his face.

"Rosetta, how lovely to see you." Frank gestured for her to take a seat.

"Mr Howard, I have been so worried about you. When I heard that you had woken up after so long, I had to bring you over some of my homemade soup."

Frank started to laugh.

"You need to build up your strength," said Rosetta, already putting the dish on the table and pulling it closer to his chest so that he could eat. Frank knew that she would not take no for an answer. He was glad at that because he had not realised how famished he actually was. Rosetta said something quickly in Spanish, perhaps a prayer, and took a seat.

In between sips of soup, Frank informed Rosetta of what had happened to both Autum and her parents, although not in great detail. As he finished, Rosetta got up and began to mumble worriedly again in Spanish, her hands flying all over the place.

"Is Mrs Howard going to be OK?" she asked, heading towards the door.

"Where are you going?" said Frank, pushing the table away and trying to sit up. Rosetta immediately turned back and helped him get more comfortable, propping him up with his pillows.

"I need to get the house ready for guests, Mr Howard. I cannot have your and Mrs Howard's parents coming home to no food! You make sure you finish that soup up, yes?" She pulled in the sheets and tucked him in even tighter and Frank laughed, remembering himself doing the same thing to Autum.

"What would I do without you, Rosetta?" he asked, pulling her towards him and kissing her on the cheek. Rosetta blushed and her Spanish went into overdrive. Frank laughed good-naturedly as she left the room.

Autum woke up after a reasonable amount of sleep. She hoped that Rosetta would not be mad that she had not let her know where she was as she had not wanted her to panic. It was too late now either way; the damage had been done. She waited for the doctors to do the rounds and when they told her that the paperwork had been signed and she was ready to go home, she was ecstatic. Her first stop was to visit her dad and see how he was getting on,

Autum stepped into her dad's room and saw that he was asleep. Her mother was not there, so she took a seat next to the bed. It was still warm; her mother must have only just left, perhaps to get a drink. Autum held her father's hand and started to stroke it. After a while, he turned and smiled at the sight of his daughter.

"Sorry, Father," was all she could say as she picked up one of his hands and placed a kiss on it.

"Shush, Autum… Lucky swing, that's all," he replied, trying to make a light-hearted joke of it.

"But you have two broken ribs!" Autum replied, not seeing the funny side.

"I would happily have had them all broken if it kept you alive." And at that, Autum broke down crying, just as her mother walked back into the room.

"Mum!" Autum mouthed and she continued to sob on her mother's chest until she was all burned out.

Autum phoned Frank and told him not to worry about her, letting him know that she was spending time with her father and that she would visit him shortly. The family talked for a long time about many things. As they talked, a nurse walked in to say that the police were there and that they needed to talk to Autum's father. Autum looked over at him and saw him nod. Two officers entered the room. They spoke to Autum and her father for an hour, forcing her to relive the details of her nightmare again. They left behind them a pain-filled father, an upset mother and a distraught daughter. When she had recovered enough, Autum left to see her husband.

On the way to the hospital, she thought about Jack lying in the morgue, about Jason and also about how Isobelle must have been feeling. There were so many people that all needed to be looked after and she just could not do it all. On arrival, she put on her best face and headed to Frank's room. Jason was already there.

"Jason! Err, what are you doing here?" She had not meant it to come out the way it had but the shock of seeing him had made her tone sound a lot worse than the situation called for.

"Just popped in to see Frank," he said. "How are you feeling?" He planted a kiss on her cheek.

"I'm fine, considering…" She went as red as a beetroot, forgetting that Jason had just lost his son. "I didn't mean that…" *Me and my big mouth.*

"I was just leaving anyway." He shook Frank's hand.

"If you need anything, just ask," said Frank.

"Thank you," said Jason and left the room.

"Come here and give me a kiss," said Frank, opening his arms to greet his wife. She kissed him on the cheek and he looked totally disappointed.

"Is that all I get?" he said, putting on his sad face and giving her his best puppy-dog eyes. She kissed him again and this time Frank held on to her tightly, prolonging the kiss. He moved his hand to grab on to the back of her head and bring her down to the bed, where she rested, wrapping both her arms around his neck. Before she knew it, Frank had eased back on to his pillow, bringing her down literally on top of him, kissing her until she broke for air.

"Now, that's better!" he said, giving her his sexiest laugh. She had missed it for so long.

"Sorry about yesterday," she said, her voice quiet.

"What's bothering you, Autum? Is it Jason?"

"Oh God, no. Well, yes and no? What I mean is that I just don't know what to say to him. I feel so bad and I don't want to make things worse by saying the wrong thing. But by not saying anything, it's even worse; it seems like I don't care, even though I do."

"Find some time and talk to him, Autum. He will understand. He does not blame you!"

"Is that why he was here?"

"No, we were just talking man-to-man; he has no one else here to talk to. I told him that I would be happy to help in whatever way I can with the funeral."

"Oh… I was unsure if you wanted to attend? After everything he's…"

"Yes, I will be there by your side" Frank's voice full of support for his wife.

"After everything he's put us through, you still want to go?" Autum was confused at why Frank wanted to do this.

"Listen to me, Autum. Jack was the love of your life." Frank lifted himself up and looked her straight in the eye.

"No, Frank…" she tried to interrupt.

"Well he meant a lot to you. You loved him enough to be his future wife. What he did hurt you, hurt both of us, but deep down he never gave up on you. I didn't agree with his actions and we know how far he had been prepared to go for the woman he loved. Jack was a lost soul and no one could have saved him from himself. It is just a shame he went to those extremes to

47

prove it. You need to say your goodbyes to him. He would want you to do that, you know he would. And then maybe this chapter in our lives can truly be closed."

She smiled up at Frank and sighed deeply. As always, he was right. Deep down, Autum knew she could not move on until she had said her piece. There were a lot of things that she had wanted to say to Jack but had never got the chance to. Not spiteful things but things she truly wanted to get off her chest. She knew that without Frank by her side she would not be strong enough on the day and was happy that she could lean on him when the time came. She would ask the doctor whether Frank would be able to come home in the next day or two and then she would speak to Jason.

I laughed when I saw the dish of soup on the table and Frank told me more of Rosetta's visit. Rooms were being made up at home for my parents as well as his. I knew his parents were flying in the next day and I needed to be there to greet them. *Wow, what an eventful few days. No wonder I'm knackered.* I stayed a while longer and told Frank off yet again for putting pressure on Rebecca to spill the beans, which he found amusing. The nurse came in and that was my cue to leave. I kissed him quickly before he could embarrass me any further and went to find the doctor. After looking for him for twenty minutes, I found him doing his rounds.

"Autum," the doctor said, sounding quite joyous.

"I'm sorry to interrupt," I said, "but I just wanted to know if you had any idea when I can take my husband home?"

"If you can give me five minutes, I will pop over and take a look at his chart, OK?"

"Thank you," I said. I hovered outside Frank's room like a naughty school-child waiting for a report from the headmaster.

True to his word, the doctor was back five minutes later. I greeted him and he went inside. He came out with the charts, making "umm, yes" and "ah-ha" type noises. *Like that is supposed to mean something to me!*

"Your husband is quite stubborn, Mrs Howard. Trying to run before he can walk, if you catch my drift." And I definitely could. "He has asked me if I can discharge him today."

"Oh boy," was all I could say in response. "I'm sorry. He isn't used to being stuck in one place."

The doctor paused for a moment, a very long one. Then he said that if Frank were able to find a nurse to look after him at home, to help him along with his physiotherapy and make sure that he did not overdo himself, he would get the paperwork ready and I could indeed take him home that day, on the basis that he stayed on the ground floor. I said that that would be fine as we had two bedrooms both with en-suite bathrooms downstairs. It would just mean that his parents would have to stay upstairs. Finally things were looking up.

"Can I quickly go in and tell him? I promise I won't be long."

"Of course you can," said the doctor and with that, he left.

I told Frank the good news and he immediately phoned Rosetta. *Poor woman has probably not stopped all day.* Once he had finished with that call, he was calling José. *Now that will be interesting: the two of them fighting it out for "Cook of the Year"!* When Frank came off the phone, I just shook my head.

"How will that work?" I said, knowing that he would understand what I was referring to.

"They have worked together before! I like for them both to help out when I entertain." I raised an eyebrow.

"Who are we entertaining in your condition? The doctor told me to make sure that you rest and don't overdo things."

"I need to get back to work."

"What the hell! No, Frank. If that's what you're planning, I will go back out there and tell the doctor to keep you strapped to that bed."

"I promise I won't do much, just work from my study, invite some colleagues over and run my business from home."

Why was I even trying to argue? He had probably put the plans in motion before the doctor had agreed to let him leave. I walked towards the door, feeling defeated. I needed to try and help Rosetta with the house, even though she would probably have none of it. I would come back later to pick up Frank.

"Autum?" I turn around and look at that stubborn, sexy man. That stubble should definitely stay, I remind myself, it adds a rugged sex appeal to that amazing face of his.

"I know Frank, I know," I say and with that, I leave and prepare for my husband to come home.

I phone my parents to tell them the news about Frank and get even more excited when I find out that my father will be released the next day. There is not much more that the doctors can do but let the ribs heal by themselves, with the aid of lots of painkillers. Looking after the two most important men in my life is going to be fun but a challenge, I'm sure. I laugh to myself, thinking of Frank. *Especially with one of them...*

I head home to see Rosetta has turned the downstairs bedroom into a full working room. Most of Frank's clothes are already in the wardrobes, his personal belongings, most of his aftershaves... God, this woman is bionic! No wonder he respects her so much. And she hasn't stopped there: most of my things have also been moved downstairs. All I can say is, "Thanks."

As I head into the kitchen I see all the work-surfaces polished, the cupboards overflowing with food and the wine rack filled with the finest wines, expensive champagnes and the best cognac money can buy. *I think he is more than "entertaining" here...* I get a call from Frank and he informs me that he has asked his PA, Tracey, to bring over some files. He asks me to let her in when she arrives. I check his study and it looks fine – *for now* – so I continue to help Rosetta, following whatever orders she gives me. Two hours later, Frank calls again, saying that he has now been released and asking whether I can pick him up. I tell Rosetta the good news and she goes into even more of a panic. Why? I don't know! There is nothing that she has not done already.

Heading back to the hospital, I wonder what our lives will be like now. No looking over my shoulder, no crank calls from Jack, no kidnapping, just my plain, old life back, if that's at all possible. Releasing a big sigh, I pull up right outside the hospital and inform reception that I am picking someone up and won't be more than ten or so minutes. Skipping along, I head towards Frank's room and see him waiting patiently in his wheelchair, with his nurse and a few belongings beside him. I try and take the wheelchair but the nurse is having none of it, so I walk alongside Frank holding his hand. We chat as we walk the short distance to the exit and once outside, the nurse helps Frank into the front passenger seat, we load up the wheelchair and Frank and I set off home.

Chapter Five

I put my hand on his leg for reassurance, something he always did for me, and he put his hand on top of mine to say he understood. It was going to be hard for him to adjust back into normal life. He hadn't missed much but I knew he would think he had. I watched how he looked around the streets as if he had not seen them before, how he pointed out some shops as if they were new. He wanted me to take him to the park so I headed there and stopped the car.

"I want to go for a little walk," Frank said

"I thought you'd want to go straight home?" I replied, a little puzzled.

"I just want us to spend some time together, before they all start fussing." He smiled and I smiled too.

"Of course," I said. As I was heading to get the wheelchair out from the back of the car, he told me to leave it as he wanted to walk. So I did, reluctantly.

As I helped him out of the car, using my body for support, I looked around for the nearest bench and we made our way slowly there, Frank shuffling forward. When we sat down, he was totally breathless.

"Isn't this beautiful?" he asked.

I looked around and took in the families laughing and playing on the grass around us, people holding hands, dog walkers and the odd person riding their bike.

"Do you think I will ever be the same again?" Frank's voice was low and his mind seemed to be far away. I looked at him.

"You are the same, Frank. Nothing has changed, you're still the sexy man I fell in love with and you're the love of my life. Is that what was worrying you?"

I took hold of his hand and kissed it, then placed a kiss on his lips.

"What about if I can't get it up?" Frank said in a whisper, looking down between his legs.

I couldn't help it, I just burst out laughing. I laughed so much that I started to cry and the more I tried to compose myself, the worse I got.

"Sorry, Frank, but of all the things I thought might be worrying you, I have to admit that was not on my list!" I continued to chuckle.

"I'm glad you find it funny, this is my manhood we're talking about here." Concerns were still clouding his face.

I got closer to him, planted soft kisses down his face, then whispered, "I cannot wait to take your dick in my mouth again, to suck it slowly, grind it against my teeth as I circle the tip around my tongue." I continued talking dirty a while longer before I bit on his earlobe and pulled away.

"Ah, Jesus, Autum, you've given me a semi!" And with that, Frank started to laugh, followed by me.

"We're going to be fine, Frank." I stood up and held out my hand for him, then headed back to the car.

They were both in a jolly mood on the drive back to the house. Frank was a proud man and had had his confidence knocked back a little. Maybe his worrying about not being able to satisfy his wife had bothered him more than Autum realised. She was just glad to have him with her. Sex was something that would happen when she thought he was ready but the way he was hurrying her to get home, it seemed that might be a lot sooner than she expected. *But hey, he is going to be disappointed. He is so dirty, I cannot believe he is thinking of sex already!* Autum chuckled to herself.

When they pulled up outside the house, Rosetta immediately opened the door, smiling. Frank's nurse had already arrived.

Autum looked at her smug husband.

"Don't expect any wash-downs. If I catch those hands where they aren't supposed to be, I will make sure that you won't be able to get it up at all!" she said, seeing how young the nurse looked.

"You have nothing to fear, wifey. Only have eyes for you." As he spoke, Frank rubbed his hand around Autum's ass, gave it a slight squeeze and laughed.

The nurse met them by the car and automatically took over holding Frank. He turned to his wife and smiled. Autum, on the other hand, had steam coming out of her ears. Why she felt so possessive, she didn't know: maybe because, even though she knew the nurse was only doing her job, she wanted to be the one taking care of her husband. Rosetta broke her thoughts.

"Mrs Howard, will your family be arriving shortly? I have prepared the room for your father."

"Thanks Rosetta," she managed to say, continuing into the house. Her parents had left a message that they would be taking a taxi and that Autum should not worry about picking them up. The house was already filling up. Autum told the nurse that Frank needed to rest and that she could take over – the nurse was happy to step aside. Frank still thought it was funny and Autum just shook her head. *He can be such a boy!* By the time Autum had got Frank into his nightwear and stopped his hands from wandering around her breasts, ass and more, he was out like a light. She asked the nurse if this was usual and she said that it was, which made Autum feel better. She left the door slightly ajar and waited for her parents to arrive.

Isobelle woke up in a good mood; she had plans for her "best friend" and her husband. She was planning on visiting Jason as well. She made her way into the bathroom and was surrounded by all of Jack's toiletries. She stopped a while to smell his aftershave, his body lotions and even his deodorant. Her stomach tightened. She started to get angry and threw his aftershave at the mirror, which smashed into pieces. The last bottle she had to remind her of Jack's scent spilled all over the floor. Once she realised what she had done, she started to cry and tried to scrape up what was left of his smell in her hands, as if it could somehow bring him back.

"You bitch, Autum. You fucking bitch," she started to mumble to herself, telling Jack that she hadn't meant to break the cabinet glass and that she was clearing it up right now. She started to talk to him as if he were there, telling him that she was going to visit his father and give him the best send-off ever. *You're going to be so proud of me, Jack. Just wait and see.* After cleaning up the bathroom, she dialled Jason's number and told him she was on her way to him. Before he could respond, she hung up. She changed into a black, low-cut dress that fell just above the knee, pearl jewellery and her killer heels. She put her make-up on to try and conceal her puffy eyes and, once she was happy with the way she looked, she headed out to see Jason.

Jason hadn't slept very well and was debating whether to call that bitch of an ex-wife to let her know that the son she had abandoned had died. But, he thought to himself, she had not bothered all these years to contact him, even to see what a success he had made of his business – nothing. Would she even shed a tear? Jason didn't think so. He started to pace as his temper started to rise. He started to curse under his breath, blaming her for so many things. If she had been a good mother, Jack would still have been living in California. If she had been a good wife, what would their lives have been like? What if this and what if that? His mind was in overdrive and he knew he needed to let off some steam. He picked up a vase, the first thing he spotted, and threw it into the wall. Then another. He took the paintings off their hangings and smashed them on the corner of the table, screaming, "Whore!" and, "Bitch!"

He heard the phone ring and paused. He just stared at it, trying to figure out who could be calling him. He dropped what was left of the painting he was holding to the floor and answered.

"What?" He was in no mood to be nice.

"There is a lady in the foyer. Says you are expecting her. She gave her name as Isobelle?" The receptionist's voice was shaky.

Jason paused for a moment and remembered that she had invited herself over without giving him a chance to speak. Another whore bitch in the making, he thought to himself.

"Send her up," he said and slammed down the phone.

He was still breathless when she knocked on the door and he let her in. The first thing he noticed was how seductive she looked in black. He wondered what game she was playing. Was she pretending to be the grieving girlfriend? Whatever her claims, she had been nothing to his son. He drew his gaze from her and walked back into the living room.

Isobelle scanned the room to see it was almost totally wrecked and wondered if she had stopped him trashing the place. Although he could probably buy the hotel outright, anyway. Maybe this was not the right time or maybe it was. A small but devious smile started to curl at the corner of her mouth.

"Jason," she said, putting her arms around his shoulders.

"What do you want, woman?" he asked, shrugging her off and walking away to pour himself a drink.

"Is this a bad time?" she said, pursuing him further.

"What do you think? What do you want?" Jason was in no mood for small talk and could not control his breathing, his temper or his mood.

Isobelle walked straight into him and started to weep, wrapping her arms around him.

"I miss him, Jason, I really do." She tried to rub her chest against his, pinning him to the spot. She continued to "cry" until she felt Jason put down the glass and return the gesture. A smile lit up that devious face of hers. She could hear his heart beating faster and she could tell that the more she fidgeted, the more he was getting aroused. She heard the groan he let escape and she seized the opportunity to lift her head up to under his neck. She too started to breathe heavily and her hot breath started to tease his ear. His hands had started to wander down her back slowly and when he reached the base of her spine she arched into him, feeling his erection growing.

"I need you, Jason," was all she whispered in his ear before he grabbed her hair, pulled her head back and took her mouth. She didn't care that he was hurting her; that heightened her arousal even more. She took his tongue in her mouth and devoured it. Their teeth scraped against each other and they worked their tongues in and out of each other and yet the force of him did not slow down. She dropped her bag on the floor as she started to strip him, tearing away at his shirt, tugging at his belt and unzipping his trousers.

Jason was hurt. He knew the kind of woman Isobelle was and at that moment, it was not that he wanted her, just that he wanted to hurt her. She was just another version of his wife, always after something better, and as he unzipped her dress, it was his wife that he saw in front of him. He was going to fuck the bitch up so badly that she wouldn't come back for more. When she slipped out of the dress, he took a step back and noticed the little satin number she was wearing. The bra just about covered those big tits of hers and the tiny thong would be snapped in seconds. *The grieving girlfriend...* He laughed to himself.

Isobelle looked at the lust in his eyes and knew she had got Jason where she wanted him. Sex was just part of it. And did she feel guilty? Why would she? After all, she was grieving. She slowly undid her bra and threw it at him. Then she took off her thong, walked up to him and moved it around his neck and under his nose before discarding it over her shoulder. With one hand, she took hold of both of his and placed them on her breasts. He squeezed them tightly before letting go. With her free hand, she rubbed his crotch, finding him fully erect. She helped him slip out of his trousers and boxers and, a split second later, they both went wild for each other.

They locked mouths again as Jason lifted her up, wrapped her around him and headed for the bedroom. He came up for air and flung her on to the bed. She smiled at him and opened her legs wide. There was no shame in what she was doing, just lust. His seed had started to spill and her eyes widened even more. When he didn't move, she sat up and moved to the edge of the bed where she grabbed his cock hard, which made Jason gasp. He put it straight into her mouth and when the heat of her hit him, he tilted his head back and let out a guttural noise. *God, this bitch was good...* Or was it just the lack of women since his wife that made him realise how much he had missed this? As he looked down, she was looking back up at him and his cock hardened even more. He again grabbed her hair and, as

60

he moved backwards and forwards, giving her more of him, he saw the look of pleasure on her face and pulled out before he came in her mouth. He knelt down and spread her legs as wide as they would go, smelling her sex before he even had the chance to taste her. Once his tongue hit her clit, she moaned loudly. She leaned back slightly and held on to the sheets, gripping them with her fists. He continued his onslaught, dipping into her then biting her clit. When she cried out in pain, he sucked it over and over again. He put his fingers in and worked that hole of hers at some speed until she clenched her thighs shut, sealing his hand there as she came. He quickly turned her over and made her go on all fours, before he rammed into her from behind, feeling her juices and her orgasm sucking him in. As she pushed back towards him, he grabbed her by the waist and ploughed into her full-throttle. As she begged for more, he gave her more, the noise of skin and skin slapping against each other. Beads of sweat ran off Jason and Isobelle as they continued to fuck. But Isobelle wanted to be in control; this was what she wanted. She wanted him helpless, wanting and needy. She pulled away from him and his mouth went to open in protest.

"Lie down," she said as she pushed him on to his back and straddled him. She knew that Jason was going to be at *her* mercy. He would be the one begging for her to stop. She had got him just where she wanted him: *under her.* Isobelle placed herself on top of Jason and slid down his cock, taking the full brunt of him. He was older but he was fit and he was big and he knew how to work a woman. As she ground on top of him, Jason lifted himself up and wrapped her legs around him so that they were both facing each other. She wrapped her arms around his neck as they rocked back and forth, back and forth. He fed off her mouth and leaned her back to take in her breast. He supported her back as he bit on her nipples one by one, sucked them hard and flicked them around with his tongue. Jason wanted to come and was bursting to do so but he wanted to dominate her. He spun her on to her back, lifted himself up and put her feet over his shoulders. He fucked her so fast and hard that they both had to find something to grip on to. Jason bent over her further and went in deeper, the angle making her cry out with pleasure and even pain. Her tits were bouncing to the rhythm of him fucking her and he bent down more to take them in his mouth. It was not long before he felt his seed rushing out of him into Isobelle and her meeting him seconds afterwards with her own. They both continued to pant for some time before Jason collapsed on to his side beside her and looked her straight in the eye.

Isobelle was fully sated. She had wanted to be in control but realised that Jason was her equal. He had wanted to dominate her too and in the end that pleased her even more. As she smiled to herself, she wondered how many more times like this she would have with him, if he let her. She felt as if she was still connected to Jack through his dad. As sick as that may seem, it was how she felt. She raised her hand to brush along his cheek but he pulled away and rose up.

"Jason," was the only word that left Isobelle's mouth.

"Get out, you whore," was what left his.

Chapter Six

Isobelle got out of bed and went to touch Jason's shoulder but he turned and walked out of the room. She trailed behind him, picking up all her pieces of clothing as she went.

"I didn't mean to come on to you the way I did, it just happened. You felt the connection just as much as I did and you know it."

"What I know is that I was weak and, like a fool, I let you seduce me," Jason responded coldly.

"Seduce you? Are you kidding me? The way you kissed me! Fucked me! It was more like you seducing me," Isobelle hit back.

"Is that what you came here for? A quick fuck?" He turned to look at her sharply.

"I came here because I wanted to be included in the funeral arrangement. He meant a lot to me."

"Yes, I can see that." And he took in her nakedness with disgust. "He meant a lot to Autum too, before you came along and ruined it. But you don't care about that, do you? You have no shame in fucking your way to what you want." Jason's lips curved as he spoke.

Isobelle had never expected that she would bed Jason, although she might have considered it when she first left her apartment. Regardless, now that it had happened, she was not leaving until she got what she came for, an alliance.

"Jason, I don't care what you think of me. Well, actually, I do. But even though you may not want to hear this, Jack was happy fucking me behind Autum's back. I didn't need to twist his arm. He knew what he was doing. He made that choice to see me. He made that choice to fuck me and he made that choice to be with me."

"I beg to differ," Jason said as he flung Isobelle's panties at her. "You see, it takes two to tango and you decided that you were quite happy for my son, who was engaged to be married, to sleep with you behind your best friend's back. You were quite happy to keep laughing in her face and not own up to what you were doing. You! Her best friend! You had a choice and you chose to play the innocent bystander in all of this. I expected more of you than that. Leftovers is what Jack settled for."

"Despite what you think, I did what I did because I loved him from day one; I was the one who saw him first."

"Yes, that might be true but, for whatever reason, he did not pick you, did he?"

Isobelle's heart sank at the thought. Jason was right and she knew it. Jack had rejected her at the beginning and no matter how they had eventually ended up, she was still second best: "leftovers", as Jason put it. That stung even more.

"I didn't kill your precious son. Remember that. I thought we could work together and take revenge on your son's killer but I see he didn't mean that much to you after all." And with that, Isobelle slammed the door and walked out.

Jason was heaving mad. He was already upset with what he had done and with whom. He had let his anger at his ex-wife add fuel to an already burning fire. He had wanted to fuck her for all the wrong reasons but she was good, whore-good. It made him even more mad. He poured himself another drink and sat down. *I'm not the one who killed your son.* That was what she had said. He tapped his fingers on his glass and contemplated his next move. Did he want to take revenge on his son's killer? Could he hurt Autum? He knew that he couldn't. He knew Jack… wasn't well. He knew his obsession. How much Jack had loved Autum had taken him a step too far. All he wanted to do was make sure that Jack was given a funeral he would be proud of. He got up to take a shower and wash Isobelle's scent off him. Then he headed to the hospital.

Jason sat with his son's body. He talked about all the things that they should have done but had never got the chance to do. He talked about how he was going to stay in England for a while and run the business until he could put someone else in charge. He explained that on the day of the funeral, the office would close for a day out of respect. Jason started to cry, thinking of all the time with his son he had lost. He cried because he would never see Jack grow old, marry or have kids. He cried because he blamed himself for not being a good father or a role model. If he had been, his son would never have left California and would still be alive today. Who was to blame for his son's death...? He was.

He left the hospital, a broken man. The body would not be released until the autopsy had been completed and the death certificate had been produced. Jason did not want his son's body to remain there any longer than needed. His phone rang and he answered it, happy that his close friend back home had called him. They spoke for several minutes but found himself drifting in and out at one point. He thanked his friend and headed for his car.

Autum had settled Frank into bed when the doorbell rang. She left to see who was at the door and was greeted by her parents. She ran straight towards them.

"I'm so glad you're here," said Autum with a smile as Rosetta helped them with their bags.

Autum escorted her father to the living room and helped him settle in.

"Do you need anything, Dad?" she asked, kissing his forehead.

"Besides painkillers, I'm fine. Stop fussing and go look after that husband of yours! By the way, where is he?"

"Resting." Autum smiled to herself, knowing that she would like him to be resting by the time she got into bed. She spent the next few hours chatting and laughing with her family. It was what she needed to bring her back to some sort of normality.

She thanked Rosetta for all of her hard work as the night was drawing to an end. Frank's parents were due the next day and the house would be complete. It was near eleven when everyone retired to their rooms…

I snuck into bed besides Frank, happy that he was still out for the count. I smiled to myself as I started to drift off to sleep when a familiar heat source surrounded me. I turned to face my husband, who had a smile on his face.

"Not going to happen tonight, dear," I whispered and kissed him good night. I smiled as I turned away and could hear Frank sigh.

The next morning came around quicker than I would have liked. By the time I entered the kitchen, Rosetta was already in full flow, preparing breakfast. The doorbell rang but it was only ten past eight, too early for Elena's flight to have come in. I answered the door; it was the nurse.

"Oh," I said, "I did not expect you here this early. Please come in." I asked her to wait in the living room while I let Frank know she had arrived but she was having none of it.

"It's OK, Mrs Howard, I can take it from here," she said, walking past me and straight into the bedroom. I found myself grinding my teeth.

I wanted to follow her but then I heard my mother calling me and my mind changed its focus. I greeted her with a kiss and ask her how my father had slept.

"He was in a lot of pain and struggled to sleep," was her reply.

"Sorry to hear that. I can get the nurse to check on him if you want?" I suggested, kissing her forehead.

"That would be nice, if only to settle him." I headed towards the bedroom.

Frank was sitting up and in his chair. The nurse looked like she was checking his heartbeat. A stethoscope was round her neck and her fingers were feeling his pulse as she checked the little watch attached to her breast pocket.

"Sorry to disturb you but, when you have finished here, could you just take a look at my father? He is still in a lot of pain and did not sleep well last night." I smiled at my sexy husband, seeing his rugged, morning look.

"I will be happy to take a look, Mrs Howard, when I have finished." She gave me that "now-can-you-leave-me-so-that-I-can-get-on-with-my-work" look and I left them alone.

I rejoined my mother in having breakfast and chatted for a while about how my father was feeling, about how I was holding up and about Jack's funeral. I still needed to speak to Jason and decided I would see him once Frank's family had arrived and settled in. After the nurse had checked in on my father and the painkillers had taken effect, my father began to sleep better. Frank, fully dressed and without his wheelchair, had moved into the living room after his physio. He chatted with my mother for a while, then excused himself and asked me to help him towards his study.

"Don't tell me you want to start working already?" I asked.

"Just checking a few emails. That's all, I promise," he replied, with a cheeky grin, as I helped him into his chair.

"Well if you need me, just call. OK?" I kissed him and started to walk away.

"Don't leave. Please."

I turned round to look at him. I had never heard desperation like that in his voice before.

"Is everything OK, Frank?"

"Just want you near me, that's all. Please stay awhile and sit beside me."

It did not take me long to reach his desk and sit beside him. I placed my arm over his shoulder and cuddled him, watching him working as if nothing had happened. After an hour, I heard a knock on the door and both his parents stepped in. I jumped up in shock.

"What are you doing here? I was going to pick you up at the airport," I said, greeting them with hugs and kisses.

"Nonsense, we would not have you pick us up. Besides, Frank had already arranged for a driver to meet us at the airport."

I turned around to see Frank standing proudly behind his desk. He used it to steady himself as he moved to greet his parents. His mother wrapped her arms around him, squeezing the life out of him, and his father hugged both of them. I caught his mother weeping and, realising that they needed this moment alone, I slowly crept out of the study.

A week passed. My father's pain decreased slightly and Frank started to walk better. He had been pushing himself hard and his memory of what had happened was still hazy but it helped that the whole family were bustling around the house. Frank worked from his study and had a steady flow of business associates coming and going. It was great. Rebecca found time to visit and so did the rest of the girls. And I knew it was time for me to go and visit Jason.

Jason was glad to hear that his son's body had been released. He had confirmed all of the funeral arrangements and needed to speak to Autum and Frank to confirm if they would attend. He had been bombarded by calls from Isobelle and had decided that, if she wanted to help, she could organise the workforce to make sure that the office was closed for the day out of respect for his son. He let her organise the flowers, the parking and the seating, which she seemed more than happy to do. She had turned up unannounced at his hotel with a list of hymns that she thought would be fitting but he had dismissed them. He found it hard to resist that sinful body of hers and she had no problem flaunting it in his face but resist it he did. She had no shame and no morals but he still did not know what she was after.

He had returned home for a few days and had been consoled by the few friends he held dear to him. He had broken down many times, looking through all of the photos of his son, trying to find the one that would be on the programmes he was having printed. The guilt of his failings as a father weighed heavily on him every day that passed. He thought of what Isobelle had said to him about him not being there and how Autum had said that Jack just wanted his father to be proud of him. And proud he was. He'd just never told Jack how much. He picked up a photo of Jack, taken just before he left to go to Britain to run his own office. He had that cheeky, confident smile on his face and had donned a tailor-made, three piece, blue suit, with handmade shoes, gold cufflinks that Jason had given him. He was very proud of his son, very proud, and he knew then exactly what his son would be wearing at the funeral. That made him smile and he picked up the phone to make some calls.

Jason's phone rang. He sighed, knowing it could only be one person. He did not even ask who it was, just told reception to send her up and opened the door in preparation. He poured a drink to steady his nerves and faced the window. When he heard the soft voice of Autum, he spun around, shocked and happy at the same time. He greeted her with a hug and a kiss on the cheek.

"I hope you don't mind me just turning up like this." Autum felt nervous.

"I wasn't sure if I would. It's lovely seeing you." He motioned for her to sit down.

"I'm so sorry, Jason, for leaving it so long before I saw you. I just didn't know what to say." Jason took her hand.

"Will you be there?"

"We both will, Jason," she replied, putting her hand on top of his.

"I'm finding it hard, Autum. Next week I will bury my son."

"In England?" Autum was slightly taken aback, thought he may have held a service but then flown him back home.

"Yes, I thought long and hard about what I should do and he loved it here. I know he would want this." He wiped away a tear. "I also need to ask you something. I know you have every right to say 'No' but would you say a few words? Please. You knew him so well and I just want to make this special for him."

71

"Jason, I…"

"Please, Autum…" *I can't say "No".*

"I need to ask you something as well, Jason."

"Anything," he said.

"I… need to say my goodbyes and wanted to know if I could visit him in the Chapel of Rest."

Jason looked up and for a split second didn't know what to say.

"Consider it done." And with that, Autum rose, kissed Jason on the cheek and left.

Autum returned home and informed Frank of how her meeting had gone with Jason.

"I'm so glad you've sorted it," said Frank. "You know this is the right thing to do but it will also be the hardest thing you will ever have to do."

Frank noticed how Autum struggled to sleep that week. It was worst the night before she was due to pay her respects. Her behaviour slightly changed and she seemed distant. But Frank's main concern was that she hardly spoke or ate, keeping her mind occupied with looking after her father and fussing over Frank's business associates. He knew it was going to be hard on her and decided to speak to her that night. The guests and Frank's PA left his office. Rosetta and José were clearing up the last of the food that they had lovingly prepared. It had been a hectic week but Frank knew everything was running smoothly and that made it all the more hard to see Autum so drained. He looked up as his wife approached him in his study.

"How was your meeting?" she said with a smile, giving Frank a kiss on his forehead.

"It went very well, darling, but let's just forget about that for the moment. Let's talk about you."

"Me?" Autum moved closer and sat beside her husband on the armrest. "I'm fine, Frank. Why do you ask?"

"You can lie to yourself, Autum, but not to me. You have not been sleeping or eating properly. I know that tomorrow is going to be hard but…"

Autum stood and tried to walk away, laughing off Frank's suggestion.

"Talk to me, Autum." Frank raised his voice slightly, stood and walked towards her. Autum stood firm as her husband's arms wrapped around her. She leaned her head on his shoulder and started to cry.

"I don't know if I can do this, Frank. I have been going over and over it in my head and I think to myself, 'What will it achieve?' I still cannot believe he is gone because of me."

"Listen to me, Autum. I will never be able to really understand what you all went through and I'm so glad that you were not taken from me. You need to go and see him and don't just remember how it ended, remember what you had together." Frank couldn't believe what he was actually saying.

"How can you say that? Don't you love me anymore?" Autum looked at him, confused.

Frank started to laugh and pulled his wife closer to him.

"It's because I love you that I ask you to do this. You need to get rid of the hold he had on you, the demons that still plague you, before you can move on, before we can move on. I know that you… loved him despite how it ended and it cannot be easy for you to detach those feelings now that he has gone. Maybe when things get back to normal, you'll consider visiting Dr Hillard again for a talk."

"You mean the shrink?" She raised her eyebrows and saw Frank chuckling to himself. Autum's voice altered as she spoke.

"Frank, I did… love him but that meant nothing in the end, once he'd cheated on me. I know a part of me, deep down, will always think of him but not in the way you may think. You're right though, I do need to do this, I do." Autum knew she had said the words but they did not sound convincing, even to her. She placed a gentle kiss on her husband's lips before she departed from the room.

Chapter Seven

Autum woke up, feeling sick at the thought of the day ahead. But she had promised that she would do this, no matter how hard it was going to be. Frank was fussing over her and brought her breakfast in bed even though she was not in the mood to eat. She took a long shower, dressed and headed out of the door. Frank had told her to ring him at any time if it got too much and she knew he would drop everything to get to her: that was the loving man she had married.

It took all her will to look at Jack's coffin lying in front of her. She stared at the elaborate decoration that surrounded the coffin. Jason had spared no expense to give his son the best before he was laid to rest. As she thought that, she knew it would only be seconds before a flood of tears finally captured her. Jack was at peace and she knew that deep down she also was at peace and that was all she wanted. She talked to Jack for almost an hour, reminiscing about the times they had had and the jokes he had used to play on her, even making herself laugh in the process. She found that her mind drifted off on more than one occasion. She found the place so relaxing that she nearly missed the gentle knock at the door. Jason peaked his head through and asked if he could come in. Autum quickly wiped away her tears and apologised about the length of time she had been there.

"I needed that," she said, as a smile lifted her features. "Thank you Jason." She blew a final kiss to Jack's coffin.

"Goodbye."

Jason was so glad that Autum had come. He knew that he too would end up looking drained by the time he left that place. Even though he had spent some time with his son a few days earlier, when he had brought his son's clothes, this, in its own way, seemed more surreal. He sat down for the next few hours, asking his son to forgive him and trying his best to tell his son how much he loved him.

Autum did not go straight home but did phone Frank, saying that she felt a whole lot better but needed some air. She drove around for a while and then went home, feeling like a whole new woman. New beginnings, she thought to herself, as she went to greet her husband.

Isobelle felt happy that she was playing a part in Jack's funeral, even though she wanted to do so much more. She had seen Jason a few times over the past two weeks to go over certain details of the funeral. He was closing down the office for the day out of respect for his son. A few employees were still in shock that their boss, Mr Jack Cartwright, had died and a few had asked his father if they could attend the funeral. Jason was more than happy for them to attend and Isobelle was in charge of making sure the venue would be large enough to accommodate all those attending. Jason seemed happy for her to make some decisions: making sure that enough programmes had been printed and organising flowers for the church and for his son's grave. Her anger had been tamed quite a bit since the incident and being around Jason made her feel *special*. She knew that they shared a bond and that bond would keep bringing them together. She did not need anyone else and that brought a smile to her face. Tomorrow was going to be the day everyone would see how much she loved Jack, especially Autum.

Autum woke up to find Frank smiling at her in bed.

"Don't you ever sleep?" she asked. She still could not get over how lightly he slept.

Frank chuckled and kissed his wife lovingly, then lifted himself on to his elbows.

"Nervous?" He knew that she had stayed up most of the night preparing her speech.

"Just need today over with, that's all." She sat up in bed.

"I'll be there by your side." He snuggled closer to her and laid his head on her stomach.

"I know you will." She ran her hands gently through his hair, her mind far away.

Frank was the first to hit the shower and get dressed, leaving Autum to take her time to get ready. As he headed downstairs, he heard his father approaching him. Frank's father patted him on the back and they talked over the breakfast bar, enjoying the aroma of the coffee and food being lovingly prepared by Rosetta.

"How is she, son?" his father said in a soft tone.

"Holding up, Dad. I just hope it's not too much for her," he replied, his voice giving away his emotions.

Frank's father reassured him as they ate breakfast. Despite his family being in the house, Frank felt as though he had not spent much time with them. He felt a pang in his chest, knowing how far they had travelled to be with him. He promised himself that he would make it up to them, one way or another. They both looked up to see Autum's parents approaching. They all greeted each other and before long the room was full of chatter and Rosetta's food was quickly disappearing. When Autum entered the room, for a split second the room felt silent. Then Frank got up to let his wife sit down, before giving her a quick squeeze and getting her a drink.

Autum knew that the atmosphere had changed and tried to smile it off as best as she could. Frank could see how uncomfortable his wife had become and gave her mother a quick look, which she cottoned on to quickly.

"Autum, can I have a word?"

Jolted from her thoughts, Autum looked up.

"Of course, Mum, is everything OK?" she replied and followed her out of the room.

Frank felt like he was lost. He had thought he could be strong enough for the both of them but he was failing miserably and they had not even left the house yet.

"Be strong, son," said his father, as if he had read Frank's mind.

When Autum returned, Frank could tell she had been crying. Her beautiful eyes were red and her mother was lovingly holding her, as if she was going to collapse. God, thought Frank, today is not going to be good. But it's time…

Jason had offered for them to go in the family car but Autum had refused, saying it was too much for her to deal with. The funeral cars were already there when they arrived. Frank got out of the car, helping Autum from the passenger side. They entered the house that Jason has rented. He couldn't have them meeting at the Ritz, could he! As they approached the hearse, Autum's gaze was drawn to the beautiful flowers that had been arranged around the coffin. That simple word, "Jack", inside a red heart and, on the other side, a second heart, with just the word "Son". Autum felt her legs go weak. Frank already had his arm around her waist but he had to stop and turn to her, wrapping his other arm around her to stop her from falling.

"Jesus, Autum are you OK? You have gone white as a sheet." He glided the back of his hand across her cheek. Before she could respond, Jason came out of the house to greet some other guest. When he spotted them, he headed straight over.

"Is she OK?"

"I'm sorry, seeing all of this just…" Autum could not finish the sentence.

They all walked into the house and Jason asked the waiters to get Autum some water. But she did not have much time to enjoy the cold liquid as she could suddenly hear the most hysterical commotion from outside that drew a crowd to the windows. *Isobelle. Who else?* She turned back round and continued to drink and compose herself. She had not seen Isobelle since they were in the hospital. *And the grieving girlfriend award goes to…* As Autum looked up, she saw Isobelle being escorted in by Jason. Isobelle glanced across at Frank and Autum and pretended to faint. *Give me strength.* Autum looked at Jason, who looked set to blow a fuse. She decided to take over and help Isobelle sit down.

"What are you doing?" said Isobelle, scowling, "I don't need your help, you murderer."

Autum looked around, feeling all eyes on her. Heat rushed to her cheeks, faster than a bullet. Frank quickly covered the distance and gave Isobelle a warning that left no room for error.

"This is not about you. This is for Jason to bury his son. You should do well to remember that." He led Autum away.

Once Isobelle's tears had miraculously disappeared, she tried to head towards Jason, who shrugged her off and continued to introduce guests to one another. He gave Frank a nod of thanks. After around ten minutes, Jason began to speak, loud enough so that everyone could hear.

"Ladies and gentlemen, it is time for you to make you way into the cars and head towards the church." Autum could see him trying to keep up his hard exterior as he spoke. She watched how his shoulders slumped afterwards, once most of the guests had gone outside.

"Frank, make sure he's OK." Frank followed her gaze and realised she was referring to Jason.

"Will you be OK with…?" he asked.

"She's no threat to me." And with that, she let Frank leave her side, watched the two men give each other a proper man-hug and walked outside.

"Watch it, bitch," she heard Isobelle whisper, pushing past her, hitting her shoulder and not even looking back.

Autum finished her drink and waited in the car for Frank to return. She saw Isobelle look out of the rear window of the family car with a grin on her face.

As they took their places in the church, Frank and Autum were given programmes and took their seats near the front of the church, where Jason had reserved a few rows for very close friends and work colleagues. As Autum looked round the church, she realised it was one of the churches in which she and Jack had thought about getting married after his proposal. She smiled inwardly at the thought that Jack was still having the last laugh. Just then, the organ started to play and everyone rose. A proud father led the procession with his friends, linking arms under Jack's coffin. As the hymns were sung, Autum kept glancing at Jason who was being consoled by his friends. The priest read a few chapters from the bible and then Frank got up to speak. He had placed a beautiful picture of Jack on top of the coffin and was explaining to everyone where it was taken. He talked about Jack growing up and had to pause a few times while he wiped away his tears. He glanced over to the coffin, explaining how sorry he was for not being the father he should have been and how proud he was of Jack's life and of the friends Jack had held dear during his life in London.

"And talking of dear friends, I would like to now call upon Autum to say a few words."

Frank gave her hand a little squeeze and told her that she would be OK and then she headed towards the pulpit at the front of the church. She had written down what she wanted to say but had read it so many times that she knew what she wanted to say off by heart. When she looked up, she could see venom in Isobelle's eyes but she blocked her out and started to speak.

"I look around here today and see that Jack would indeed have been proud of the turnout. Jack knew how to live life to the full and always talked of the love he had for his father. He often said how nothing he had achieved in life would have been possible without his father's guidance." She looked up to see tears rolling down Jason's cheeks. She could feel teats on her own face too. "Jack would not want us to be sad and would only want us to celebrate the good things he had done in life. I hope he knew that we did have some good times together." Autum fell silent and then made her way down from the pulpit, pausing to kiss Jack's coffin before moving to offer commiserations to Jason.

"Thank you," said Jason.

"I meant every word I said, I hope you know that," said Autum. A smile lit up Jason's face.

"I know you did and that gives me peace of mind."

Before the priest could even announce her, Isobelle got up and made her way to the pulpit. Her dress was so tight that she struggled to climb the few steps. She dabbed her eyes for effect before she began to speak.

"I'm sorry that we have all been brought here today to see a father having to bury his son, who was taken from him in such horrible circumstances." She looked straight at Autum. "For those of you who I have not yet had a chance to meet, I was Jack's fiancée." Jason's head shot up so quickly he nearly lifted himself off the bench. Frank and Autum felt similarly shocked. "I loved him so much and it hurts so bad inside. It's still hard to believe that he has gone. Rest in peace, my love, and don't worry: God will punish those that took you

82

away from me and your father." And with that, she left the stage, head held as high as her heels, with no remorse for her lies. If God punishes anyone, thought Autum, it won't be me. As the service came to a close, the organ started to play again and Jack's coffin was loaded and taken away. Jason had bought a private plot and only wanted a handful of people to attend the burial. The rest were told to make their way to the reception. Autum and Frank waited for the coffin to be loaded into the hearse and followed closely to where Jack was going to be laid to rest.

"You did well in there," said Frank in the car, his hand resting on Autum's knee.

The reception room was beautiful, with a large picture of Jack at the front of the room, just before the stage. Jason took the microphone, thanked everyone for their kind words and told them that he wanted to celebrate Jack's life. He flicked on a projector and pictures of Jack appeared, from when he was a baby up until a few months ago. Autum was so shocked. She did not realise that Jack must have been sending his father pictures of himself whilst in England. Some were of the two of them together. She nearly choked on her drink.

"God, Frank, I had no idea he had all these pictures." Her voice was shaky from the shock.

"Look at him, Autum. Look how happy these pictures are making Jason feel. These are his memories to treasure." And with that, they continued to enjoy the reception as Jason had wanted, with music softly playing in the background. A few hours later, it was time for them to say their goodbyes.

"Autum," said Jason as they left, "I apologise for what Isobelle said in the church. We all know that Jack never proposed to her."

83

"You have nothing to apologise for, I'm not sure who she was trying to convince but we all know the truth and that's what matters." She gave Jason a kiss on the cheek.

"Will you be staying around for long?" Frank asked.

"About a month. I need to hand over the running of the office to one of my closest friends until I can find someone whom I trust to take over permanently."

"Well, don't be a stranger. Call us if you need anything and thanks again." Frank gave Jason another man-hug and a slap on the back.

"Oh, I nearly forgot to say: be careful," Autum said in a whisper.

"Of who?" Jason clearly was puzzled.

"Of her." They all glanced around to see Isobelle, a glass in her hand, staring intently at them.

Chapter Eight

Frank and Autum's life was slowly getting back to what could be classed as normal. Two weeks had gone by and Autum was still waiting to see if she was going to be charged with murder or indeed charged at all. Isobelle had taken two weeks' leave and was due back at work soon and both Frank's and Autum's parents had travelled home. Autum couldn't believe how quiet the house seemed after all the noise of the last couple of weeks. It was nice to have the house back however and Frank was making good and steady progress, with the nurse still coming round to make sure that he was keeping up his physio.

Autum wanted to spend some quality time with her husband and organised a weekend away at Frank's lodge in Lincolnshire, a place that brought back memories, good and bad, for her and a place where she always felt at peace. She wanted to get back on track and start trying for another baby. She had already been for a check-up and was recovering well.

"Hurry up, Frank, I want to leave early to avoid the traffic," said an ecstatic Autum.

"God, I've never seen you so happy," said a chuckling Frank.

Little did Frank know that his wife planned a weekend full of sex and nothing else. During the drive, Frank took a few calls, much to his wife's annoyance, but when his phone rang again, for the umpteenth time, Autum held out her hand and told Frank to hand over the phone, like a mother scolding a child. Frank ignored the gesture and put it back inside his jacket. Autum glanced at him, just catching the sly grin that was lighting up his face. *We'll see how long that lasts.* Autum grinned back and saw frown lines appearing on Frank's forehead. He couldn't read what was going on in her head and that made her smile spread even more. The drive to the lodge was pleasant and joyful. Their conversations covered a range of topics and every so often Frank found that his hand had wandered to his wife's thigh. It didn't help that her dress looked long when she stood up but way too short when she sat down. When Frank tried to move his hand higher, Autum slapped it away and said she needed to concentrate on the road.

It was lunchtime when they arrived at the lodge and Frank unpacked the weekend bags. When Autum got inside, she noticed that José had already been and gone and left them a note saying that he had prepared a light lunch for them and left a selection of wines and desserts.

"What!" said Frank, raising his hands with a chuckle.

"I can cook, you know? If you give me the chance," Autum replied, shaking her head. "Does this mean José will be back this evening?" Frank smiled.

"You know he loves to cook," he responded as if that was his get-out-of-jail-free card. "He will be here around six-thirty." He opened the wine and started to take the platters out of the fridge.

Autum took the bags into their room. She only had a few hours before José was due to come back: a weekend might seem like a two-day break but, before you know it, it is time to go back to work and Autum wanted to make sure they had a good break. She unpacked the bags, slipped into something "a little lighter" and headed back upstairs.

Frank was relaxing on the sofa with a glass of wine in his hand. He did not see her approach until she sat on the sofa beside him. She sipped her wine as Frank shot up from his slouching position to take a good look at his wife. His eyes scanned over a black, low-cut bra, a skimpy, not-worth-putting-on G-string, stockings and suspenders and some killer, black heels. She was staring right at him, still sipping her wine. It was only when she parted her sexy thighs that Frank nearly forgot what it was like to breathe. Autum put a finger in her mouth and sucked it, she then traced the outline of her nipple and pinched it, then she spread her legs even more and moved around her G-String and inserted her finger, never breaking eye contact from Frank, who just about managed to place his glass on the table with shaky hands before he got up and approached his wife, nearly forgetting how to walk, he felt that weak. It had been a long time since his manhood had seen some action, as Autum had refused any sex while he was recovering. Every night, it had nearly killed him to smell her sweet perfume, see her in her underwear and sleep beside her, knowing she had his best interests at heart. And now, it looked like that torment was over.

"Keep that finger where it is" as he stretched out to touch her beautiful skin, his mouth started to water at the thought of joining that finger, he bent down as his hands held her thighs open, then his phone started to ring.

"Damn it," he said, turning his head in the direction of the noise and starting to walk. Autum got up faster and retrieved the phone before him. It was Frank's buddy David, with whom he played golf.

"Hey, David, how are you?" said Autum, as Frank held out his hand for the phone. She backed away and continued to talk. "Yes, Frank is here but he can't get to the phone right now. Would you like me to pass on a message?"

Frank took another step forward with a plea on his face, whispering, "Give me the phone," but all Autum did was stop him with a killer heel right in his chest. He could gather from the conversation that she was repeating back to him that if he was up for golf tomorrow then David would pick him up. Again Frank tried to move.

"Sorry, David, but Frank and I are having a weekend of sex and he will not be in any fit state to play golf." She hung up the phone before David could even stutter, "OK."

Frank's mouth stood open and even as he watched Autum turn off his phone and throw it on to the sofa, he did not budge. It was only when she removed her heel from his chest and moved towards him that he tried to speak. But he was slow and Autum filled that space with her hot lips. As she invaded his mouth with her tongue, Frank went wild. He wasn't sure if it was the combination of the lust he was feeling for his wife for not having been able to touch her but his fuse had definitely been lit. His body was trying to explode before he could even use it. Frank had never stripped so fast in his life. As he backed his wife towards the table, he knew that there would be no foreplay. He needed to be inside her quick. As he lifted her up and pushed the chairs away from the table, he broke their kiss to look at her and smiled, slowly stripping her of her G-string, leaving everything else in place.

"Frank," was all Autum had the chance to say before his cock slammed into her wet pussy.

"Jesus," was his reply, before he continued his onslaught of hard thrusts. As both their groans merged into one, he grabbed a chair and sat down.

"Are you OK?" said Autum, taking stock of a breathless Frank.

"God, yes!" he laughed, "just a little bit out of practice, that's all!" He grabbed her and she straddled him.

His tongue licked up and down her neck and he nipped her earlobe, as she ground into him. He grabbed a breast and sucked as much of it into his mouth as he could. He flicked her hard nipple then bit it, hard enough for her to moan with pleasure as she felt no pain. She lifted herself up then slammed herself down on to Frank's cock, as he grabbed hold of her ass. She rode him relentlessly, up and down, her breasts rubbing hard against his chest.

"Fuck me, Frank! Fuck me!" He pulled her off himself and carried her to the sofa. He didn't mean to but he almost threw her on to the sofa, before taking her from behind.

"How I've missed this!" he said as he slowly entered her, his cock just a mass of hard muscle with no intention of going down. He spread her legs and went deeper. As she gripped whatever she could, he picked up his rhythm. She felt droplets of sweat hit her back as he leaned down to kiss her spine, his fingers circling her clit as she pushed back.

"Harder!" she shouted, his balls smashing into her from behind sending sensations to her clit. As she lost control and climaxed, she could feel his cock getting harder, thicker and wider, before he exploded with a loud moan and collapsed on top of her. They both stayed there for some time before he turned her around and they cuddled up together on the sofa and fell asleep. It was only when they heard a knock and a key turning in the door that they both bolted up. Autum headed for the stairs but Frank quickly threw on his trousers before José walked in. There were clothes, shoes – the lot – left in their wake. Autum was going to let Frank explain this one and took a quick shower to freshen up.

José walked through the second door to see Frank, bare-chested and gathering clothes under his arms. It didn't take a genius to figure out what was going on.

"Should I come back a bit later, Mr Howard?" was all José could say as he scanned the scene in the room.

"That won't be necessary, José. You just carry on while I pick these up," said Frank who felt no shame at what had just gone on.

"It's nice to see you well again," said a chuckling José.

"At least I know that everything seems to be working OK!" Frank tried to make a light hearted joke of it.

"You take your time, Mr Howard. It looks like I will need to reset the table anyway." He pointed to the dishevelled state of the table and chairs with his cutting knife and began to chop vegetables, mumbling something about young love.

Frank now felt conscious of the state the room was in. He was glad that his loving wife had not seen her husband nearly lost for words. He felt happy like he could deal with anything. As he headed towards the stairs, he continued to pick up the remaining clothes, including a scrap of underwear under the table that he hid in his pocket, chuckling. When they reappeared for dinner, the room was smart again and Autum knew that she would not be able to look at José without blushing. Autum was famished, having not had lunch, and praised José for his cuisine. Dinner was chargrilled veal served with new potatoes and a mixed leaf salad, with crème brûlée for dessert.

"Thank you," said Autum, and meant it.

"You're welcome, Mrs Howard!" José replied, tidying away his utensils.

"Would you like me to come in a little later in the morning?" he said to Frank.

"No José, your normal time is fine. Sorry you had to see… you know…" He trailed off as Autum kicked him under the table, as he smiled.

"No problem, Mr Howard, Mrs Howard," said José and, with that, he bid them goodbye and left the lodge.

"Men…" was all Autum could say, as she shook her head and began to finish off her dessert. But Frank was getting his mojo back and was ready for round two: no sooner had José left than he walked over to his wife and turned her chair towards him. She knew that look and knew that her brûlée was not going to get finished.

"I love you so much," he said and bent down to kiss her, his hands stroking both her thighs, as he kissed her mouth heavily, his tongue capturing the taste of the crème brûlée. Her breath quickened with the force and when he parted her legs, a moan escaped her.

"Take off your skirt." She did as he wished but not fast. She was enjoying the look he was giving her, the way his eyes followed her every move and the way his breathing was telling her he wanted more. She stood up, knowing her panties were wet, and her arousal went up a notch. He looked at her and pulled them slowly down until she stepped out of them and sat down. He grabbed one leg and placed kisses up to her thigh before placing it on his shoulder. Then he did the same with the other one, pulling her closer to the edge of the chair. He leaned in and she arched her back as the heat of his tongue lapped around her clit, flicking and sucking as he built up his speed. His fingers found her entrance and slid gently in, one after another after another, until she was gripping on to the edges of the chair, her heavy breathing letting him know she was too far gone to speak, too far gone to move and far to gone to care. It brought a smile to his face as his fingers plunged in and out. He stopped for a while and pulled out and she let out a sharp breath and looked down at him, at herself and the way her legs were sprawled over his shoulders. All she wanted then was more of what he was doing, more of what he was giving, just more…

"Don't stop," she whispered

"Greedy, aren't you, wifey?" he said, lifting himself up and taking her mouth, her juices all over his tongue. He wrapped her around his body and moved her to the sofa.

"Stay there," he said, disappearing downstairs and returning with some blankets and pillows. She started to laugh, removing the rest of her clothes as he did the same. When he tried to continue where he left off, she reluctantly stopped him. Her hands wrapped around his cock before any words left his mouth and he felt her hot, sexy mouth taking him all the way to the back of her throat. His cock felt hot and moist inside her mouth, making his knees go weak, as he watched her head go up and down, up and down. He felt the force of his cock being sucked in as he ran his hands through her hair.

"Suck me harder." He realised it sounded like a plea but he didn't care. "Yes, oh God, yes." He gripped her hair tighter and began moving his hips to the rhythm of her sucks. She looked up at him and his cock twitched in satisfaction. She smiled, pulling him out of her mouth with a popping sound to run her tongue over his tip as he started to spill. His lack of sex had been driving him insane and when he watched how the tip of her tongue came out to lap at his tip he spilled some more. He laid her on her back and teased her by rubbing the tip of his cock around her entrance and her clit. The friction made the low noises coming from her mouth all the more pleasing. As he continued to rub her up and down, she tried to raise her hips up for contact. He could feel her juice spilling out and inhaled a breath, needing to be inside her. His cock entered her at force, but slid in so gentle, she was that wet, knocking the air

93

out of her. She felt like he had grown in size. Or was it just the lack of contact over the past few months that made her pussy seem so small? God, she was feeling dizzy, excited and dirty all at once. He grabbed a pillow and put it under her ass as he went deeper. He leaned in to take her breast into his mouth, to bite and suck it. He wanted to do it all. She was squeezing him and the friction was driving him insane. He wanted to come so badly but he needed her to come even more so he decided to go more slowly, pulling out just to the tip then slowly going back in again, over and over. He began to build his speed back up until he heard her cries and felt her pussy drawing him in even more. Everything he had he gave in those seconds and his cries seemed to take over hers. He felt the mixture of their warm juices flow in between them as his body fell to her side, his cock still inside her. They fell asleep where they lay.

Sunday arrived all too soon and it was time to head back home. They both felt more than sated and Autum was looking forward to spending some more time at the office in Birmingham as she felt she had missed out on a lot since the initial set-up. When Frank checked his phone, he found some amusing voice messages from his friends David *and* Peter, who he knew would not let this drop, and a few from his associates. He smiled to himself; his sexy weekend was truly over and it was back to business as usual. Once home, Autum called Rebecca to prepare for the next day. *Monday is going to be a long day…*

Isobelle went to visit Jack's grave every day and vowed to keep her promise of revenge. She had wanted

Jason to be a part of it but the man was too much of a pussy to help and had now returned to California without even saying goodbye. *Bastard.* She felt stronger now and knew that this was a lone crusade that only she could complete. This was going to be it. She just did not yet know what *it* was going to involve. Jason was letting her stay in his apartment while he decided what to do with it, so for now she could relax and still be around Jack's belongings. She had felt so good when she announced that she was Jack's fiancée. She knew that it was hurting both Jason and Autum but she didn't care. She had no one left and had lost her few remaining friends to *that bitch*. She thought how good Frank had looked at the funeral and how well his recovery was coming along. She laughed hysterically, thinking how Autum had it all. She stayed by the grave for an hour, talking to Jack, she mentioned the turnout at the funeral, the hymns that were played and the beautiful flowers people had bought, she mentioned how his father had said how proud he was and how at the reception everyone saw pictures of him from a child to when he ran the business, "they all loved you Jack" just like me. She ended by asking him to help her plan her next move.

Monday came and she put her best face on and went back into work. She was pleased that at least some of the office staff had given her cards and some flowers on her first day back, sending their condolences. Their kind words made her emotional. At lunchtime she went to her usual café and spotted Rebecca.

"How is Autum holding up?"

"She's doing fine," replied Rebecca suspiciously, as she continued to walk out of the café.

"I did love him, you know?" Tears filled Isobelle's eyes as she blocked Rebecca's path.

Rebecca was unsure how to react. Was Isobelle being genuine or was this some sort of trick?

"I'm sure you did and I'm sorry for your loss. It was a shock for all of us." Rebecca shifted from foot to foot uncomfortably.

"Thank you," was all Isobelle said as she headed for the counter, leaving a bemused Rebecca behind.

By three in the afternoon, Isobelle had made her way to Frank's office and asked his PA, Tracey, if she could have a quick word. This time, she did not burst in but sat outside and waited for Tracey to announce her. After a few minutes, Tracey confirmed that she could go in.

"I just wanted to have a quick word, if that is OK?" said Isobelle, standing in front of Frank's desk. He gestured for her to sit.

"What's on your mind?" he said, in a harsher tone than he had intended.

"I just wanted to know if we can try and move on, try and be civil, at least, to one another and put all this bad blood behind us."

"Listen, Isobelle, these past few months have pushed us all to the limits and I'm sorry at the outcome. We have all been affected by this, one way or another, and I am happy for us all to put this behind us, if you mean it." He cast his eye over her, trying to read her body language.

"I do," she said, smiling gently. "Well, that is all I wanted to say, Mr Howard." And she got up and held out her hand so that he could shake it.

Frank was taken a bit off guard at this gesture but he stood up and leaned across his desk to shake her hand. She smiled but seemed reluctant to let his hand go. He did not want to be rude and pull it away.

"My hand?" he replied.

"Oh, yes, forgive me." She let it go and walked out of his office. What Frank could not see was the big smile that had lit up her face. Her scheming had now started to take form.

Chapter Nine

Frank left the office, still a bit fazed by the events of the afternoon. He had expected Isobelle might come in with some cock-and-bull story or some drama involving Autum: just… anything. Except that! He knew that a leopard would never change its spots but *this* felt scary. He decided to ring Rebecca to find out if anything unusual had happened to her in the office that day. He was shocked to find that she had also been approached.

"Do you think she's playing some sort of game?" asked Rebecca.

"Who knows? But what more could she gain from this?" Frank replied.

"Could she have spoken to Autum?" Rebecca asked.

"I doubt it. I would have heard about it by now," Frank said.

"At least that's something, then." She let out a sigh. "Are you going to tell her?"

"No," he responded instantly.

"I don't know, Frank. This is Isobelle we're dealing with, remember that."

She was right: they were dealing with someone who could change in a split second, rotten to the core. He felt bad thinking it but no good could ever come out of anything Isobelle said or did.

It was nearly eight by the time Autum got home. Frank was relieved to see her. He tried to act like nothing was bothering him but the way he grabbed hold of her and kissed her in the foyer, like he was about to lose her, set alarm bells ringing.

"What's going on?" she said, as she pulled away from his lips.

"Nothing. Just glad to see you home," said Frank, going in for round two.

"You're not hiding anything from me, are you, Frank?"

"Of course not, honey." He could feel his heart nearly beating through his chest and decided to change the subject.

They talked, while they ate dinner, about both of their days. He watched how full of excitement her lovely face was when she talked about the office in Birmingham and he knew then that Isobelle had not tried to make contact with her. Rosetta was still in the kitchen when Frank got up and nibbled Autum's ear, making her blush. Autum looked in Rosetta's direction and Rosetta flapped her hands, reeled off a lot of words in Spanish, mumbled something about "young love", gave a little laugh and said simply, "Go and make babies." Autum went bright, rosy pink.

"You heard the woman," said a chuckling Frank.

Autum knew she always battled to contain Frank's amusement when he got like this. And he loved to do it even more in front of Rosetta.

"Get upstairs, unless you want me to nibble on more than your ear in the kitchen," he whispered in Autum's ear.

She didn't know where to look, just said her good nights and left the room, vowing to kill Frank when he got upstairs. Frank could not stop laughing as they entered the bedroom but Autum had no time to challenge him before he had pinned her to the back of the door her back towards him, arms held in place above her head and her face away from him. The first thing she felt was how hard he had become in such a short space of time: he was pressing his erection into her ass. Her breath quickened and tingles started to work their way all over her body as he gave her a slight poke. He pulled her hair to the side and started to nip at her earlobes and lick up and down her neck. Then he placed a trail of kisses from her ear down to her shoulders.

"I hope you're not tired?" he said as he pushed back into her making his cock feel like a sword, his breath hot against her ear.

"Worn out," she replied, pretending to yawn.

"You will be," he said, as one hand worked its way slowly down the side of her dress and back up. He wrapped his fingers around her panties and slowly pulled them down.

"Don't you move," he said, letting go of her arms so that he could remove her panties entirely. Then he unzipped her dress, brought her hands gently down to her side and placed kisses gently on her back. Autum automatically opened her legs wide for him.

"So dirty," he said, lowering himself and licking her up from the inside of her legs to the top of her thighs, smelling her sweet wetness. He grabbed hold of her ass, giving it a quick squeeze and holding on to her tightly as he sucked and nibbled on her clit. Her knees nearly buckled under her and she moaned.

"Frank," she said, looking down at him, her voice broken.

"So wet," he said, still working his tongue. Ignoring her moans, he inserted his fingers with an onslaught of thrusts. Frank was now as hard as stone. His balls felt like lead weights and his trousers were tight and uncomfortable. He pulled out his fingers and begun to strip, hearing her gasp for breath, made him strip that much quicker. He spun her around too quickly and she nearly lost her balance, her head dizzy with pleasure.

"Oh God, Frank, just take me, will you!" She unclasped her bra and threw it on the floor.

One sight of his wife, naked, panting and wet was all he needed. He put his hands each side of her head, pinning her to the door, and kissed her hard, full of passion and lust. She could taste herself on his tongue, bitter, sweet but sexy as hell. His cock pressed hard into her stomach. Her hands in his hair, she pulled him closer. His hands found her breasts and he grabbed a handful and rubbed them. He pinched her nipple, hard enough to hear her cry out, making his cock rise even more. He guided his cock to her entrance, as she tried to rise up on to her toes to push herself on to him. Want, need, love and desire took over and he pushed hard inside her, slamming her back against the door as he cried out with the need for his woman. His heavy breathing rushed past her ear and his tongue lapped at her face, sweat encased them both.

The room was filled with the banging noise of Autum's body hitting the door, her heavy breathing and her cries for her husband to go in deeper as she bounced harder on to him, the air smelt of sex plus so much more. She wrapped her hands around his neck and tightened her legs around his hips. Her nails dug into his back as she arched, his cock, now even harder inside her, she was sealed in place, nothing strong enough was going to break through. As she came close to her climax, she took his mouth but he pulled away.

"Look at me, I want to see your beautiful face when you come around my cock" he said and, with one final hard thrust, she came hard. He could feel that rush inside her, see how her eyes tried their hardest not to close as her face glowed with satisfaction, she was milking him, urging him to follow, sucking him into oblivion as he continued to drive her wild. Then, before long, he followed her, shooting everything he had inside her with a high-pitched growl until his thrusts finally slowed down. He carried her then to the bathroom, still embedded in her, her legs firmly wrapped around him. They let each other go and showered together, laughing, before finally going to bed.

Autum woke early the next day for work, feeling her aches and pains from the night before. She smiled to herself and hummed as she prepared herself for work. She tried to take a quick shower but with no such luck as Frank quickly joined her. She hoped that he had no intentions of ruining her before work but by the time he had lathered her body, covered it with kisses and then left her wanting, she knew she would be a very frustrated woman. He could hear her calling him back to the shower as he started to get dressed, chuckling.

"Glad you found that funny," she said, tugging her towel tightly around her body.

"Don't know what you're talking about," he smiled, raising an eyebrow.

"Men," she said, trying not to touch the parts of her body that were making her tingle, which was not working. Her poor hair took most of the frustration and ended up looking like a tangled mess. She watched Frank in the mirror, still smiling to himself. All she could do was nod her head and smile too: Frank was definitely making a full recovery and more.

Isobelle had been enjoying work and was putting in a lot of hours, as she didn't want to go back to an empty apartment. She realised how quiet and lonely she really was and she had no friends to take some of that away. Why was everyone around her looking so happy? Why did everyone seem to have friends? And why was it that her stomach tightened when she thought about Autum and Frank? How, despite everything they had gone through, were they so full of love and happy-looking? She wanted some of that. She knew that Autum was running the Birmingham office and came back late most nights. She also overheard Rebecca talking about another "girls' night in" that Friday, which meant that Frank would be home alone. Isobelle was planning her own special party, which would involve only her and him.

It was now Thursday night and Autum arrived home around nine. She was too tired to eat and found Frank hard at work in his study. She gave him a quick kiss and retired early to bed. She was glad it was nearly Friday: soon she could let her hair down and take some girlie time out with Rebecca and friends. Boy, did she need a drink after the week she'd had! She did not realise how tiring all that travelling could be, combined with coming home to amazing sex night after night. Her poor body was totally sexed out. Once Friday arrived, Autum made her way to Birmingham as usual. She was glad that she was only doing half a day. Her bags were packed for her overnight stay and Dionne, Emily and Imogen kept the phone calls coming, making sure that drinks were going to be plentiful. When Autum got to Rebecca's house, she noticed that they all seemed a bit overdressed for staying in.

"What's going on?" she asked in an exaggerated voice.

"It's Friday night and we thought we would hit a few bars first, then come back home," said Rebecca.

"That's not fair, I'm not dressed…" was all she managed to say before Dionne pulled out a little red dress from behind her back.

"Hurry up," she said, flinging the dress in Autum's direction.

"You've got ten minutes before we leave," said Imogen, swigging from her can then burping.

"Imogen," they all said in unison and she just started to laugh.

Ten minutes were up. Autum wasn't happy that she'd had to rush but was still pleased with the results. She reapplied her make-up and took her hair out of her ponytail and gave it a good shake. Then she scrunched it up a little and applied some of Rebecca's hairspray: job done. Emily had lined up five shots and they all clinked their glasses before knocking them back. What a great way to start the weekend, Autum thought to herself, as they linked arms, headed outside the apartment and waited for the cab to arrive. It only took fifteen minutes to reach their destination, a small but lively bar that had every drink possible as well as food. They looked at the cocktail menus first: since they were there for happy hour, they were going to make the most of it. They laughed when Imogen ordered a pint of lager. *So ladylike.*

Isobelle had just finished cleaning the house and had filled the rooms with scented candles. She had uncorked the wine and let it rest at room temperature. She did not want to look too slutty, so was wearing a knee-length skirt and a red blouse that didn't cling too tightly to her breasts. She wanted to throw him off guard. That was her plan. If she got him to come in the first place. When she looked around, she was happy with what she had accomplished. She headed into the kitchen and screwed off the old fashioned taps. Then she loosened the bolt that controlled the flow of water. She was shocked to see how quickly the damn thing got out of control. She tried replacing the taps, as water was flowing out like a river bursting its bank, but it barely helped. She dialled his office number, knowing he still had not left work yet, or rather, hoping he hadn't. Panic started to set in. Her hair, blouse and face were being pounded by the flow and he still had not picked up the receiver. Shit. What the hell had she been thinking? She was about to hang up when she heard him answer.

"Frank Howard." She had to stop herself from laughing.

"Frank, it's Isobelle," she said, letting out the odd yelp.

"What do you want? I'm busy," he replied abruptly.

"I need help. My taps have burst and I cannot seem to stop the water. Please, Frank, I wouldn't ask but I have no one else that can help me and it's too late to call out a plumber." She emphasised the desperation in her voice, although she was actually starting to panic.

"Just turn it off at the stopcock," he sighed.

"I cannot take my hand off the bloody tap to find it!" she screamed back. "Help me. Please." The phone line went silent for what felt like a lifetime and he finally said,

"I'll be there in a minute but if this is some fucking, sick joke, you'll be sorry." He wanted this warning to be clear; he was in no mood for her games.

"Phone Autum and tell her where you'll be! Phone the police! I don't care! I just need your help. Do you hate me that much?" She was praying that he didn't. Again the silence was killing her.

"I'm on my way." The line went dead.

Isobelle glanced at her phone, her eyes wide. Then she just stared into thin air. Her breathing had changed. She felt nothing then but the desire for revenge. She smiled crookedly and looked at the glass that she had left in the kitchen for him. *If he accepts it...* The water was far from her mind. Even though her hand was going slightly numb from the cold, she didn't even flinch. She was in another zone and Frank was heading straight into it.

Chapter Ten

Autum was having the time of her life. Considering they had meant to stay in, the evening had turned out even better than expected. The night was still young and the cocktails were being replaced nearly faster than they could drink them: "Sex on the Beach", "Black Russian", "Tequila Sunrise"… to name but a few. Then Emily decided to start just picking drinks with names she thought were funny: "Dirty Fucker", "Orgasm", "Blow Job"… And she didn't even care what was in them. Well, in fact, none of them did. They downed each one, scrunching up their faces, sticking out their tongues, stomping their feet madly and shaking their wrists at bizarre angles, then lining up another as soon as the shock wore off.

"Thank you, girls," was all Autum could say as they clinked glasses yet again. Imogen had moved on from lager to ale. *How does she do it?* When the real cheesy music came on – *yes, you know the ones* – Autum grabbed the other girls for a dance. *We all may deny we do it but when "Living On A Prayer" hits the speakers, your hands shoot up in the air and you start singing at the top of your lungs. Yep, I know you're smiling as that memory comes back to you.* It was now eleven at night and, without any proper food, Autum could feel her stomach telling her that if she took one more sip of her drink, the contents of her stomach would be saying hello to her shoes, hair and clothes.

It was nearing midnight when they all got back to Rebecca's. They had already stopped off at the local Chinese to pick up food but Rebecca still kept saying that she needed takeaway pizza as soon as she was home. Imogen was saying how amazing cold pizza in the morning tastes. *Yuck!* They were swaying and humming songs they didn't really know the words to, making far too much noise and, *the all important thing*, carrying their shoes in their hands: *some things never change*. They all felt less sick and tired once back at Rebecca's, crashing on to the floor or the sofa and diving into their food.

They spoke about work (*can you believe that!*), about everyone's plans and about Rebecca and Julian's relationship.

"Are you going to move in together?" someone asked.

"We've not talked about that," said Rebecca. "Just enjoying the ride for now. He's good for me."

The girls watched Rebecca's mind wander off to Julian. She smiled.

"Care to share?" said Dionne, raising an eyebrow.

"Share what?" said Rebecca, coming back to reality.

"Share wherever you have just been!" Dionne replied but Rebecca just shook her head and smiled.

110

"Shall we play spin the bottle?" said Emily.

"No!" they all replied in unison, then burst out laughing, except Imogen, who realised it must be a private joke.

It was nearly four in the morning before they all fell asleep and all Autum could do was think of her husband. She wondered whether he'd stayed up working in his study or actually had an early night. She should have phoned him but it was nice knowing that not hearing or seeing him would make her hunger for him even more. She fell into a deep sleep.

Frank hung up the phone in his office after speaking to Isobelle and wondered if he had done the right thing. She sounded desperate and he could detect the panic in her voice but was it real? He sat back in his chair for another five minutes, tapping the desk with his pen and debating what he should do. He had promised her. And what harm could she do? He dismissed his worries, grabbed his jacket and headed out of the office. It wasn't a long drive and he reached the apartment in no time. He pressed the buzzer and waited patiently.

"Frank, is that you?" Before he could answer, he heard the click of the door and he let himself in. As he walked to the apartment, a wave of emotions hit him all at once. He remembered when he first went there, after Miami: the destruction that he and Julian had found when they entered the apartment. The living room furniture had been ripped to shreds, the plates, glasses and bottles all smashed to pieces in the kitchen. And then the bedroom… his mind trailed off. A flash of the charity ball event came into his mind next and, for a split second, he remembered how he had tried to seduce his wife out of her dress before the ball. Then the scene changed and he saw her lying naked on the floor, her dress ripped to shreds by *him*. Then he thought of the last time he was here, an emotional wreck, after Jack's father had taken Autum. A screaming noise jolted him from his memories. The door was open and when he looked straight ahead, he could see that Isobelle was soaked through. At first he just stood there, still lost in his thoughts, and then she shouted his name. He flinched back to the present, took off his jacket, flung it on to the sofa and headed straight into the kitchen.

"What took you so long?" was all she could say.

"The stopcock is usually located in the cupboard under the sink, especially with these new builds," he said, as if those facts were enlightening her.

"I don't give a fuck where it is. Just find it and shut the damn thing off!" she replied, looking at him.

"Move then." He knew he sounded on edge, his memories still hovering around in the back of his mind.

She let go of the tap and when he bent down the water spayed on to his back. Moving with urgency, he spotted the damn stopcock and quickly turned it until the flow stopped completely. But by then, Frank's back and hair were soaked. When he stood up, he glanced at Isobelle. She was also soaking wet. Her hair was stuck to her face and her blouse clung to her body, revealing how low-cut her bra was underneath, her breasts overflowing it. Frank turned and walked away.

"Thank you," she said, as she tried to pull the material from her body, "let me get you a towel."

When she had left the kitchen, he turned back to the tap to take a closer look but felt her back beside him.

112

"Here," she said, handing him a towel. He noticed that she had slipped on a t-shirt and some jogging pants. He also noticed that she wore no bra.

"Thanks," he said. He gave his head and his back a quick rub down then handed her back the towel.

"Get your tap sorted," he said and started to make his way out of the kitchen to pick up his jacket.

"Can't you stay for one drink? It's the least I can do to say thanks." She joined him in the living room, keeping her distance.

"I must go but thanks for the offer."

"Please, Frank, just one? It would make me feel so much better." She could see the doubt in his eyes and heard him sigh.

Frank looked at his watch. Although it wasn't late, he did not want to be in this apartment: too many bad memories. The leak *seemed* genuine. So even though he wanted to be rude, he knew he'd feel bad doing so. He accepted the drink.

Isobelle informed Frank that there was a spare glass on the table in the kitchen and told him to just bring it in. Frank thought nothing of it because *he* fetched the glass and *he* poured out the drink. He topped up her glass and made sure she drank first. When she did, he relaxed a bit and took a few gulps from his own glass before setting it down. He didn't even notice the few tiny drops of clear liquid that had been in the bottom of his glass.

Isobelle kept Frank talking for another thirty minutes and was surprised how relaxed she felt around him. He seemed to have let down his guard around her. Nevertheless, she kept her distance and was surprised when he took the wine and topped up his glass. She noticed that he kept pinching the top of his nose and that his body had started to slouch into the sofa. She knew the drugs had started to work and a pang of guilt clenched her stomach. Deep down, she knew Frank was the good guy but anyone linked to Autum she wanted to hurt. That included Rebecca and those bitches she used to call her friends, Emily and Dionne. They all needed to pay, one way or another. Casualties were bound to occur with what she had planned.

"Frank, you look tired. Maybe you should go home," she said.

"I think you're right," he replied. He tried to get up but he lost his balance.

Isobelle shot up from where she was to help steady him and he gripped hold of her for support.

"Something doesn't feel right. You've drugged me, you bitch. What did you give me?" He tried to right himself but failed.

Isobelle smiled and held Frank under his chin so that he was facing her.

"How could I have drugged you when we both drank from the same bottle?"

Frank's head was woozy and he could not think straight but he knew that she had done something to him; he just couldn't piece it together at that moment. He bent down to pick up his jacket and his leg gave out.

"Why, Isobelle?" he said, dragging out his words.

"Sorry, Frank," was all she could say. And she actually meant it.

She sat him up straight as she started to undress, first taking off her top and straddling him. He tried to push her away with his hand but failed. Her hands ran over his face. He is so handsome, she thought to herself. She could not bring herself to kiss him. She started to unbutton his shirt, then slipped off him to undo his belt and pull down his trousers. She wanted a baby, someone she could love and look after. He wouldn't be able to prove she had drugged him. His argument would be weak and no one would believe him. She stroked his cock through his underwear. He moaned and she looked up at him.

"Lay back, Frank, and let me do all the work." She hovered her fingers over his fine hairs, then slowly slipped his boxers down. She gasped at how huge he was.

"You're such a lucky girl, Autum," she said, as her hands glided over his cock and a moan slipped from her mouth.

Frank felt like he was having an out-of-body experience. He knew something was happening to him. He could feel the touch of a woman and he knew deep down in his mind that he had not left Isobelle's apartment. But he could not move, could not focus and could not speak, only mumble and groan. Every time he tried to move, his body wouldn't react and yet hot hands was stroking his cock, making his body jerk in response, even though he had given it no permission to do so.

"Oh God, Frank," was all Isobelle could say, as her hot mouth sucked him in. She moved her mouth hungrily up and down him, not knowing how long the drug would last. Her hand cupped his balls as she fed them next into her mouth. She felt Frank move but she continue her onslaught on his body, the body that was not hers to take. She didn't care.

115

Frank was getting aroused even though he fought as hard as he could to resist. He tried to focus his mind to do something to protect himself from her but it was no use. His vision was blurry. He thought he heard the bitch say, "Sorry." She would be. He was scared that he was going to black out and never wake up and that's why he needed to keep awake, to fight it, to try and fight her for Autum's sake. He needed to do this. For his own peace of mind, he had to do this. Her mouth was hot around him. He tried to pull away but he did in mind only. He was slipping away and he wanted to cry, to scream and to kill the bitch. He wasn't the violent type and would never hit a woman but Isobelle was not a woman, only someone evil and evil had no boundaries, as he was finding out. He saw her rising to her feet and he thought that she was done with him, now she had proved her point. But then she straddled him and he knew what her intent was. She was trying to take something that was not hers to take. She was trying to destroy him as a man. She was trying to take away his dignity and he couldn't stop her.

Isobelle stopped sucking when he was nice and hard. She was getting carried away with just doing that and could have easily let him come in her mouth. But that was not what she wanted; she wanted his sperm inside her, wanted to feel him come *for her*. She just wanted to feel, to touch and to taste a man again. She stripped naked and mounted him. When she lowered herself on to him and slid on to his cock, she couldn't help but arch her back with the sheer pleasure she was getting. She placed her hands around him to steady herself as she gyrated her hips and moved up and down. Her mind had gone and was replaced by pure pleasure. A sheen of sweat covered her skin.

116

Frank realised he was being violated in the worst possible way. He felt her riding him and heard her moans as she tried to push her tits into his face. All he wanted to do was throw up. His body made attempts to move, to fight, but it made no impact at all. When he tried to move her arms from around his neck, she just moved his hands away. The bouncing up and down helped his mind to stay alert but that made no difference. The noises were getting louder in his ears and he knew she would be coming soon. But he also knew that he could not stop himself coming either and that sickened him. Patience, he told himself, she will pay...

Isobelle felt her whole body shudder with her orgasm and whimpered into his ear. She continued, feeling his cock harden inside her and knowing he was going to come. She felt the warm heat inside her and heard a muffled sound from his mouth. She stayed on top of him for some time before she climbed off and stood there, staring at him.

"Thanks, Frank," was all she said, a smile lighting up her face. Then she casually turned her back on him and walked to the bathroom to freshen up.

When Frank opened his eyes he was sitting in his car.

What the hell, he thought, as he slowly took in his surroundings... He was in the car park back at work. He checked over his attire and he was fully clothed. Nothing seemed out of place except he knew otherwise. His breathing seemed OK and his hands felt a bit shaky. It was because he felt afraid. Autum would never forgive me, he thought. Then he thought of vengeance. What did Isobelle think he would do once he came around? And, more to the point, what was she expecting him to do? His heart started to beat faster as he got out of his car and entered the building. He said hello to security at the front desk before heading to his office. It was two in the morning and when he checked his phone there were no messages from Autum.

"What's the fucking point in calling the police?" he asked himself. After the shenanigans of the last few months, he actually knew how his wife had felt the first time Jack had raped her. He knew now why she did not want them to know: the shame, the humiliation of talking about it to strangers, the disbelieving looks. No, he wasn't going to the police. Then he thought about telling Autum. Would she want to be with him still? Would she understand? He poured himself a drink from the cabinet, not caring whether whatever was in his system would be made worse with spirits. He took the decanter back to his desk and contemplated what to do next. By the time he had finished thinking, the decanter was empty and he lay sprawled out on his office desk, glass still in his hand.

Chapter Eleven

Isobelle couldn't believe what she had accomplished. She was still pumped up with adrenaline. And Frank's seed, she thought, laughing to herself. She knew Frank was a proud man and she was banking on that. Despite that, she still feared he might come back and kick down her door at any given moment. She had got the neighbour to come round to help carry Frank back to his car, saying that he was a friend that had had too much to drink and that she didn't feel safe with him in her apartment. *Showing a bit of cleavage always goes a long way.* She had dropped him back at the office and walked home, giving her some time to clear her head. She washed and dried Frank's glass and put it away. Then she headed back to her room to finish off the bottle of wine. She was quite tired when she finally drifted off to sleep with a smile on her face.

Frank stirred around six-thirty in the morning, straightened his back and stretched. He quickly got his jacket but left the decanter and glass on the table, knowing Tracey would clear it away on Monday. When he arrived home, he was greeted by Rosetta, who took in the state of him.

"Everything OK, Mr Howard?"

"Yes, Rosetta, I just worked late and forgot about the time." He rushed upstairs.

"I will prepare some breakfast for you and Mrs Howard," she replied, shouting as he disappeared.

He hit the shower quickly and enjoyed the hot water lashing at his body. No matter how long he stood there, he didn't feel clean but he knew he had to get out. As a towel hugged his hips, he gathered up the clothes he had taken off and put them in the wash basket to be thrown away later. He joined Rosetta in the kitchen and enjoyed a hearty breakfast, before heading to his study. He needed to work to take his mind off things and that's just what he did.

It was late afternoon when Autum's bubbly voice echoed through the hallway. She easily found Frank in his study, after dropping off her bags upstairs. He greeted her with a kiss but she noticed that it wasn't forthcoming, the way it usually was.

"You're not mad at me, are you, Frank?"

"What? No, why would I be?" Frank pulled away without realising how quickly he did so.

Autum tried again to kiss her husband and this time he stopped her by gripping her by the shoulders.

"I'm sorry," was all he could say before he walked out of his office, leaving a stunned Autum behind.

Autum quickly took stock of what had just happened. She had never seen Frank like this and although she tried to think of something that she might have done, she couldn't. She decided to confront him and find out what the hell had happened since she left him yesterday. She ran up the stairs to the bedroom where Frank was pacing up and down.

"Look at me, Frank."

"Autum, please, I can't do this right now," he said, without looking up at her.

"Do what, Frank? What have I done?" She stepped towards him.

Frank looked up at her and let his emotions take over.

"She..." was all Autum heard.

"She? Oh God, Frank..." She sat on the bed, put her hands on her face and started to cry.

"It's not what you think, I promise you."

"Who is she? What have you done?" Autum's words came out broken and erratic.

Frank approached the bed, knelt down and cupped his wife's chin but she shrugged him off.

"Autum, please," was all he could say.

"Did you sleep with someone?" She moved her hands to see his expression and when he didn't answer and bowed his head low, she did what most women would do... she attacked.

"You fucking bastard!" She lashed out for his face and he fell backwards to the floor. She pounced on him, raining blow after blow as he tried to fend her off.

"It's not what you think. She told me she was in trouble. I debated for ages if I should help her. I was already at the office when she called..."

"You slept with someone from the office! How could you!" Another round of slaps headed straight for his face.

Frank could take it no more. He was upset, she was upset and he still could not bring himself to tell her until she said words that left him speechless:

"I hate you, Frank." She climbed off him and headed towards the wardrobe to fetch a bag.

At first he just lay there, watching her, as if in slow motion, seeing her arms yanking clothes off the rail, draws being thrown open and every now and then, her looking back at him, full of hate. He watched her mouth moving but nothing was registering in his ears, just silent noise. Then he blinked and the loudness of her screaming was deafening. He slowly pulled himself up and snapped out of his daze when he saw her heading for the door. He shot up and, in his haste, literally ended up pinning her to the door, her head falling back hitting it.

"What are you doing? Let me go!" she screamed, trying to get out of his hold.

"Don't leave me. Please. Just let me explain."

"How could you? After everything we have been through? How could you?" The last words she spat out at him.

"You hate me? How do you think I feel? I hate myself for what she did to me." He let her go and turned his back as he continued to speak, hoping she would not bolt through the door. He could hear her breathing heavily.

"I was working late in the office when the phone rang. At first, I thought it might be you, so I was shocked to find out it was *her*."

"Who, Frank? What was her name?"

"It was Isobelle." He turned slowly to see Autum screaming and charging at him.

"For fuck's sake, Autum, listen to me!" He grabbed her by the waist, threw her on to the bed and held her there. He felt hurt and she refused to look at him, continuing to cry.

122

"She said she had a leak..."

"I bet she did!" said Autum, laughing hysterically.

Frank paused for a bit, took a deep breath and continued.

"She said that she had a leak and she was begging me for help. She was screaming down the phone and sounded desperate. I told her it better not be a trick or she would regret it. She told me to call you or the police if it would make me feel any better. I could hear the noise of water in the background and thought that she might actually be telling the truth, so I went.

"You never learn, do you?" was all Autum said, without looking at him.

"I remember approaching the hallway and how it made me feel, going back into that apartment. The first time I found you, the knife in your hand…" He trailed off. "Then, again, when I walked in and saw you naked on the floor…" Without realising it, he had let her go, and sat at the edge of the bed.

"When she opened the door and I went in, she was soaked and she was holding the tap to try and stop the flow of water. I didn't move at first until I heard her screaming at me to turn the water off. After the water stopped flowing, she left the room and I tried to look at the tap to see what might have been the cause but she came back into the kitchen with a towel so that I could dry my hair. I was about to leave when she asked me if I wanted to have a drink to say, 'Thanks.' And still I suspected nothing. She told me there was a glass on the kitchen table and I picked it up. I poured out the wine and watched her drink it first. Even then, I only had a glass or two, nothing to make me black out."

"What did you just say?" Autum shot up and joined Frank at the end of the bed.

"She started to talk to me, just general chitchat, nothing heavy. After half an hour or so, I felt funny, a bit dizzy and light headed. I tried to leave but slumped on to the sofa." Frank felt sweat on his brow. He wiped it off and stood up, walking towards the window.

"The next thing I feel is her… touching me. I was too weak to stop her. She did things to me that I am ashamed to talk about but will never forget. I brought this on myself for thinking she would have changed. She is still the devious bitch that we know. I don't know how but I must have blacked out completely as when I woke up, I was in my car in the car park back at work. I couldn't go home, didn't want to, so I just went into my office and drank myself into oblivion. I woke up at six-thirty this morning and came home, hoping that a shower would clear away the filth, the shame, the disgust. But no amount of water would wash away how I feel. So you see, Autum, there is nothing more you could say to me right now that I don't already feel. I let an evil bitch rape me and I feel less of a man than I have ever felt." He didn't even wait for Autum to acknowledge his words; he just walked out of the bedroom, got his jacket, walked out to his car and drove off, to wherever his car would take him.

Chapter Twelve

Autum sat on the bed still in shock at what Frank had just told her. *How could I have been so stupid as to think he would cheat on me? Isobelle… How many lives is she trying to destroy? How many lives will be broken by her?* Autum realised that she needed to let Frank know that she was sorry for ever doubting him, that she loved him and hoped that he would forgive her. By the time she left the bedroom to look for him, he was gone. She tried desperately to contact him by phone but it went straight to voicemail. *Oh God, Frank, where are you?* She tried ringing his close friends but they had not heard from him and she didn't think they would lie to her. She rang his office but he had not turned up at work either so she decided to give him some space to see if he would return later. Autum was angry at herself for being so stupid. She wanted to pay Isobelle a little visit. Just to talk, she tried telling herself but she knew her way of dealing with that bitch would involve punching, hair-pulling and a lot of screaming. With everything that was hovering over her, however, she knew that would not be a great move to make and that Isobelle might even be hoping that's what she'd do. *Your days are numbered, bitch.* She needed to clear her head and sought some comfort in ringing her parents. When she heard her mum's cheerful voice, she broke down, telling her everything. After forty minutes of motherly talk and advice, Autum felt calmer and much better. She decided to keep herself busy and went on her laptop to catch up on some work in Frank's study, taking the occasional break to eat. Rebecca had phoned to see if her and Frank wanted to meet up for dinner but she made her excuses and Rebecca didn't suspect a thing. They chatted for around ten minutes but Autum's heart was just not absorbing what was being said. It was only when Rebecca said, "So you agree then?" and Autum automatically said, "Yes," that Rebecca started to laugh.

"So you agree that Julian is a jerk?"

"Oh God, no. I just…"

"It's fine, I just knew you weren't listening as you kept saying 'yes' all the time."

"Sorry. Still recovering from yesterday," said Autum, hoping it sounded convincing.

"No worries. Speak to you later." And with that, Rebecca hung up.

Autum continued to work until her eyes started to burn. She realised she had been in the study for over six hours. She knew now why Frank sometimes lost track of time; it was easy to do. She rubbed her eyes and relaxed back in the chair, putting her feet up on the table. Before she knew it, she had fallen asleep.

Frank retuned home just after midnight. He had spent some time in the park, looking at all the happy couples, children and goings-on and he had felt the emptiness beside him where his wife should have been, holding him. He tried playing golf, thinking that he could let off some steam, but it just gave him more time to think. Then he went out for dinner but he couldn't eat. The restaurant was full of people with friends and loved ones and sounds of laughter echoed around him. He was all by himself. He decided to just stay in his car until he was ready to come home to an empty house. He expected that his wife would have left him. He didn't even go upstairs because he was too afraid to confirm that he was right, so he headed straight into his study, a place he loved, a place that held so many memories. As he stepped through the door, the first thing he noticed was a long pair of legs stretched out on his desk, her bare feet just waiting to be tickled. As he walked in further, he saw how lovely Autum's locks looked, flowing down and covering her face. Her hands were crossed over her stomach and her chest was rising and falling slowly as she slept. He wanted to wake her, to run his hands all over that body, suck those beautiful nipples, making her moan, and part those thighs, ready for his tongue to lick that wet pussy of hers. A smile came to his face and he felt his cock twitch with acknowledgement but then he thought that she wouldn't want him anymore, now that he had been touched by that woman. It broke his heart. He walked around his desk and placed the softest of kisses on her forehead, then went to leave.

Autum was stirring in her sleep when she smelled his scent and her body started to react. She knew he was near. At first, she was scared to open her eyes in case it was just a dream but she did. She saw him, his back towards her, heading for the door.

"Frank!" She swung her legs from the desk and stood up.

"I didn't mean to wake you. You looked tired. I wasn't expecting you to be…" He didn't want to finish. She would know what he had meant to say.

"I'm sorry for ever doubting you, Frank, it just took me by surprise, that's all." Her voice was low but he knew she was telling the truth.

"I'll always love you, you know that," he said, as he continued to walk to the door.

"Do not take another step towards that door." Autum's voice was stern and she saw Frank turn quickly towards her.

"Why do I always get drawn to this room? Tell me, Frank." She slipped her t-shirt over her head and threw it towards him.

Frank raised his eyebrows and looked at the top lying on the floor a few feet in front of him. He looked up again and marvelled at those beautiful breast just waiting to be released from that bra.

"I love this room because this is where you like to fuck me, isn't it?" She slipped out of her jogging pants and, again, threw them at his feet.

Frank felt his whole body coming to life, his heart was beating faster, his breathing getting erratic. And boy, how did the word "fuck" sound so goddamn sexy coming out of her mouth?

"I would fight for you forever, as long as you still loved and wanted me, Frank." She put her hands behind her to unclasp her bra, then dangled it between her fingers, before letting go, watching Frank's eyes following it drop.

Frank's eyes focused on his wife's breasts. He licked his lips, thinking of all the things he could do with them, if only his bloody legs would move.

"I need you, Frank. My body needs you." She turned her back on him and slowly took off her panties. When she turned back round again, she noticed how hard Frank had got, the defined line showing clearly in his trousers. She removed the laptops from the table and placed them on the floor, then swept her hand across the table, letting everything else crash to the floor, never taking her eyes off Frank. Then she moved around to the front of the desk, her hands sweeping the top as she moved.

Frank watched this goddess of a woman strip naked in front of him. He took in the way her body moved as she cleared everything off his desk. He watched how her breasts bounced off the table and how her nipples scrapes the surface. She wanted him to fuck her on that desk. She wanted him and his heart was filled with joy. He tried to adjust his pants, his cock trying to find an escape route but his balls weighing it down. He loosened the buttons on his polo shirt, feeling like it was trying to choke him. He pulled it over his head, her gorgeous eyes watching him. He took off his belt and unbuttoned his trousers. The zip was next and then he let his trousers drop to the floor, stepping out of them, his legs now deciding to work. He felt his cock push further up his stomach and gave it the freedom it was searching for. He pulled down his boxers and it sprung free, weighing heavily, as it stuck out, bouncing happily towards it prey.

Autum continued to watch as her husband slowly approached her. Her sex ached and she could feel herself getting wet. She leaned back so that her ass rested on the edge of the desk then spread her legs.

"I want you to watch me come Frank" as his eyes followed her fingers down, down and in as he took in a breath" her eyes intent of fucking him with just that look.

Now Frank was in front of her, watching how she was working her fingers in and around her pussy. *when did she get this dirty* he thought to himself as his cock told him he didn't care just wanted to fuck her dirtiness even more.

Autum didn't realise how dirty her mind was getting but she loved it, rubbing her clit and feeling it swell around her fingers knowing that her husband was going to feast on her all-inclusive buffet made her juices flow even more. She increased the pace as she watched Frank devouring her as he stepped back to take in the view.

"I want you" said Frank

"Tell me what you want to do to me" Autum replied.

Frank gripped his cock and started to rub it up and down, coating it with his own juices that had escaped.

"I want to fuck you everywhere, in everywhere. I don't want you to be able to walk, I want to see you crawling on all fours just so that I can fuck you from behind, I want to fuck your mouth until you choke and then fuck you some more. I want to feel you suck me dry and leave me weak, and I want my tongue in your pussy fucking you when you come, so that I can suck your juices dry, that's what I want."

As Autum listened to what Frank wanted she closed her eyes and fucked herself even more, he was watching, waiting to pounce and he wouldn't need to wait much longer.

"Frank" her orgasm exploding from her on a whisper as she continue fucking it out of her body.

She reached out to touch his face with her hand and watched how he closed his eyes smelling her sex over her fingers.

"Take me, Frank," was all she needed to say. His look turned into one of lust and his lips smacked into hers, taking her mouth by storm, hot, powerful and determined to cause havoc. His tongue wrapped around hers like a vine, not wanting to part. His hands found her breasts and he squeezed and pinched them. He broke from the kiss to devour her breasts one by one, sucking, tasting and biting those pink, ripe nipples until she moaned. He felt her hands in his hair as she pulled him lower. His tongue licked down her stomach and back up again. He kissed her hard, delving deeper into her mouth, then pulled away and nipped her earlobe before sucking it, his hot breath against her ear sending shivers down her spine. She felt herself being picked up as he held her tight and moved her so she was lying longways across the desk. The coldness hit her and she arched her back. He slid her down towards him and her legs went around him. His hot tongue was hitting her, making her tingle all over. Her hands grabbed his hair again as she ground herself around his mouth. He looked up at her, as she pulled herself up on to her elbows and watched him lap her up. She watched him smile as his right hand moved towards her entrance and she felt his fingers slide in. Then her head went back. The tip of his tongue was flicking her clit and then he was sucking it. His fingers were fucking her just like she was fucking herself not long ago, slowly at first,

131

and then he picked up the pace and was fucking her hard, one, two then three fingers thrusting in and out. Her body started to tremble, as the onslaught continued.

"Frank," she cried out as her orgasm took over her so quick after the last one but harder, stronger, wilder. He felt his cock starting to spill as he felt her muscles sucking at his fingers and he continued pumping in and out of her. She was still riding out her climax when he pulled out his fingers and pulled her off the desk. He wrapped her legs around his waist as his cock plunged deep inside her. He let out a gasp her pussy was so hot and wet, her arms were leaning on the edge of the desk as Frank hammered into her. She could not describe it any other way. She felt like the desk was moving backwards with the force of his thrust. He leaned in to suck her breast and she tried to keep his head there with one hand and her balance with the other. Frank stopped abruptly, still wedged inside her, to look at her face. She was flushed all over, panting and covered in a sheen of sweat.

"God, I love you, Autum." He gave her a loving kiss.

"Then show me how much," was all she said before that look of lust took over him once more.

He pulled out of her for a split second to turn her away from him and towards the desk, her ripe ass staring at him. He stroked it up and down before giving each cheek a hard slap. The exoticism of her moans filled his ears and he parted her legs further. He lifted her ass higher before plunging into her again. She slid further on to the desk as he gripped her hips hard, the beads of sweat dripping down his face. His hands and body were clammy but he knew his grip would be firm. Every time he thrust into her, he made a low guttural noise. He reached for her clit and rubbed it up and down and from side to side, he knew it was swollen and knew it was sensitive but he couldn't stop, couldn't be gentle, she was going to be sore and ache and smell so much of sex and he smiled. She was pushing back on to him and his cock hardened. When his balls slammed into her, he felt like they were grenades waiting to explode. He felt how swollen his cock was, knew the veins around them were protruding out ready to burst and knew this orgasm would kill him if he did not let himself go soon. But he fought hard to keep going; he wanted her to come again and she would. He pulled out of her and felt himself gasp for air as he caught his breath. He led her down to the floor where he lay on his back and she straddled him. She guided herself down on to his cock, his knees bent as he raised himself up to pump inside her. He gripped her waist so she would come down hard on him. She leaned in to kiss him and her breast slid across his skin, her nipples grazing his body. He was close to bursting and bit the inside of his cheeks to distract himself. It was only when she started to bounce on him and he could see that she was ready for release that he gripped her even tighter and gave one almighty thrust lifting his hips right off the floor. She screamed out, her head flopped down, her wet hair covered her face and now he could find his own aching release. He felt his whole body convulse with the sheer intensity of his orgasm. He could feel his seed shooting out from his body at a force and speed that he had never experienced before as he pumped harder and harder until he was drained, his hair and body soaked. It left him feeling like the happiest man alive.

Chapter Thirteen

When Isobelle went back to work on Monday, she was feeling smug. She wanted to see if Frank was moody, miserable – anything. What she did not bank on, however, was seeing him laughing and smiling with his staff, shaking hands with her boss before heading into the meeting room on her floor. *Is this an act for work?* She wasn't sure but it pissed her off. She had thought he would challenge her in front of witnesses so she could cry out harassment but instead he seemed unconcerned. After a thirty-five minute meeting, she saw him heading her way and she smiled, with a few jitters in her stomach.

"Morning, Mr Howard. Did you have a good weekend?" A smile lit up her face.

"Good morning, Isobelle. I had the most wonderful weekend with my wife. Thank you for asking. I hear you're doing a fantastic job here. Keep up the good work." He patted her on the shoulder and walked off, the smile disappearing from his face once he knew she could not see him. He unclenched his fist and breathed a sigh of relief as he headed to his office.

"What the fuck?" was all Isobelle could say to herself as she watched his back fade from her view. *Was that meeting about me? What is he planning to do to me this time? Why is he in such a goddamn good mood? And did he really have a good weekend with her?* All these questions were going around her head, ones she had not thought about before. She did not know much about how the drug worked but if he had no recollection of the night, even better. She laughed to herself and continued with her work, humming as she did.

When Frank reached his office, he was sweating with fear and the urge to wipe that smug look of her face. He had seen the slight panic on her face when he approached her, which meant she was scared. *Get used to it, bitch. You ain't seen nothing yet.*

Autum was back in Birmingham and had had a very enjoyable but very sore weekend and that made her smile. She and Frank had spent most of Sunday talking about what they should do next. All she knew was that Frank wanted her to act as if nothing had happened. If she saw Isobelle, she should be pleasant towards her, which she knew would be very hard. "Throw her off her game." That's what Frank had told her and she would try. Frank phoned her often, as if he were checking she had not bailed on him. But she was going nowhere. She would be home late that day, however, to make up for leaving early on Friday. No matter how much work she caught up on, it just never seemed enough.

Isobelle was still reeling from her earlier meeting and decided to take her chances with speaking to Rebecca.

"Hi, Rebecca. Can I have a quick word, please?" The painted-on smile was evident on her face.

"Make it quick. I'm busy." Rebecca did not even raise her head to acknowledge her.

"Frank is in a good mood today. Has he won over a new client or something?"

Rebecca raised her head at the odd question.

"Frank is always in a good mood, unless someone upsets him." She looked Isobelle in the eye as she said "someone".

"He told me today that I was doing a good job, after having a meeting with my boss. I just wondered if you had heard anything, that's all."

"You doing a good job?" Rebecca burst out laughing. "Yeah, right. You sure he didn't mean you did a good job of sleeping with your best mate's fiancé? Or that you did a good job kicking her in the stomach when she was pregnant? Or did he mean you're doing a good job at just being a bitch?" Rebecca looked her in the eye before dismissing her with her hand.

"How dare you say that to me? Despite what you think of me, I am very good at my job and he did praise me, thank you very much." And with that, she stormed off, her face flushed with rage.

When she had disappeared, Rebecca rang Frank's office and asked for a quick meeting, as she did not want to say anything over the phone.

"Is everything OK, Frank?"

"Yes, why? Has Autum said something?" He hoped that she had not, no matter how close she and Rebecca were.

137

"No. Should she?"

"Where is this going, Rebecca? You know I am busy."

"Isobelle came to see me, asking why you were in a good mood."

Frank burst out laughing.

"Did she now?" He continued to chuckle. "I had a great weekend, that's all. Can't a man come into work happy?"

"I'm sorry to have disturbed you. It just seemed a weird question for her to ask and I was unsure whether something had happened that I didn't know about."

"Nothing has happened, Rebecca, nothing at all. Now, unless you want me to keep my clients waiting, I really must go." And with that, he gave Rebecca a look politely telling her to leave. For the rest of the day, Frank had never felt better. His meetings gained him some new clients and another trip abroad was on the horizon. He was not going to be without his wife.

Two weeks later, Autum and Frank were boarding a plane for California. The business trip would last no longer than two days. They had arranged to meet up with Jason and he was meeting them at seven for dinner.

The sun was hot, even as the evening was settling in, and I was glad to be wearing a light, long evening dress, two inch heels and minimal accessories, my hair pinned up so that I could cool down. Frank, as always, was immaculate in his Armani blue suit, with the two top buttons of his shirt undone. We knew that Jason had expensive taste and wanted to blend in well.

Arriving at the hotel, we were escorted to a private room that Jason had hired out. When we spotted him, I noticed that he had aged a little since we had last seen him. *Because of me.*

Frank and Jason greeted each other with a man-hug and handshakes and Jason gave me a kiss on the cheek. It was like we were all trying to avoid one subject and the room fell quiet.

"How is everything?" said Frank, finally breaking the ice.

"Everything has been good here," Jason replied.

"You're looking well," said Frank unconvincingly.

"Well, I have my ups and downs, you know? About everything." He left it at that and so did we.

Frank changed the subject altogether and they talked about something they would always have in common: work. Between courses and drinks, I watched the two of them laugh and exchange conversation. It got far later than we had planned on staying, so we agreed to meet up in the morning and spend some more time with Jason before heading back home.

Like clockwork, Jason's chauffeur picked us up at eight in the morning. You could feel the weather getting warmer. California was indeed a beautiful place, from the little we saw of it, and Frank promised we would come back again and spend more time there on holiday, not for work. We were meeting Jason at his office, Cartwright Industries. The building was huge and went up almost as far as the eye could see.

"Wow," was all I could say.

"Impressive," was Frank's response as he held on to my hand and we entered the foyer. Frank did the introductions and a call was made. The receptionist then took out a special fob key, swiped it across the entrance to the lift and told us to press floor thirty-five, which we did. There were so many tall buildings, even the room in our hotel was on the forty-fifth floor. And the lifts were so quick and smooth, it didn't even feel like you were moving, which was very weird. The elevator opened and we walked out into a grand, open space and were greeted by another receptionist.

"Mr and Mrs Howard? Jason is expecting you." She led us past glass-doored meeting rooms. They were of different sizes but all were grand. They had oval-shaped desks, huge flat-screened televisions, leather seats and video-conference screens. Every single one had breathtaking views of the city. I didn't realised we had reached our destination until I bumped into Frank. The receptionist opened another set of grand doors and we stepped through.

The view was the first thing I focused on, as I heard the men greet each other. Then I looked around the room; it took my breath away. Jason really did work hard for what he had and I admired him for that. A trolley came in with tea, coffee and pastries and even though we had already had breakfast, it was nice to tuck into something sweet.

"The view is breathtaking, Jason," I said, pouring myself a cup of tea.

"Thank you, it is great. That's what attracted me to this building in the first place. It gives me so much inspiration when I look out. It calms me down when I'm having a bad day and you can never get enough of it. I see something new every day that I did not see before."

"You're a lucky man, Jason. You've worked hard for this." We talked about the building and his staff and then Jason mentioned sending some business contacts Frank's way.

"You don't need to do that," I said, trying to get up from the leather sofa as gracefully as possible. It was like it was calling me to sit back down, it was that comfortable.

"Well, I have given Frank all the details via email…"

"Email?" It shocked me slightly that they'd been contacting each other without my knowledge.

"Is something wrong?" asked Frank, walking over to me.

"No, I just didn't realise you and Jason were doing business, that's all." I felt myself blush, knowing I was overreacting to nothing.

"As I said before, Autum, they are just contact details. Frank doesn't need to follow them up if you don't want him to."

Both men were staring at me, as if waiting for some sort of reply.

"That's kind of you, Jason, thank you," was all I could say, as I sat back down on the sofa and sipped my tea.

Later on that morning, Jason took us on a whistle-stop tour of the area and showed us his home, before seeing us off at the airport.

"Thanks for the tour," said Frank.

"My pleasure, it really was good seeing you both." He kissed me goodbye and shook Frank's hand.

"I'll be in touch soon about the business contacts," said Frank.

As we relaxed in the VIP lounge, I reflected on how the trip had gone. It was great being in California. The weather and the people were wonderful, as were

141

the houses, if you could afford them. It was nice to get away, even though it was a business trip. Frank always seemed to be able to get a lot done in hardly any time. That's what you can do if you plan ahead.

"What did you think of that view in his office?" I asked, snuggling up to him.

"All I can say is that it makes my office look like a cupboard." We both laughed.

Chapter Fourteen

Isobelle had not slept very well over the last two weeks. She couldn't understand why Frank was behaving the way he was, why Autum had not challenged her. *Unless she doesn't know.* She sat up in bed, wondering what her next move should be. Should she meet up for lunch with Autum and let it slip that Frank was round her house during her sleepover? That thought was quite appealing – just to wipe that damn smile off her perfect face. It was Wednesday when Isobelle sent Autum an email.

Hi Autum,
 I hope you are well. I was wondering if you would like to meet up for a drink sometime soon, when you are not working in Birmingham. I know you said we could not be close friends and I won't push that but I would still like to see you to say hello. Let me know what you think.
 Isobelle

Autum had been in meetings all morning and when she checked her emails she noticed one from Isobelle. *What does she want now?* As Autum opened her email, she had to laugh to herself. *You're so predictable, bitch.* She picked up the phone and called Frank.

"You know she is going to tell you what happened, don't you?" She could hear the concern in his voice.

"I know, Frank." Autum spoke softly to reassure her husband.

"She may make things up. You know I don't remember much, just that I couldn't stop her from…" Frank couldn't finish what he wanted to say.

"Don't do this, Frank. Nothing she can say will surprise me, I promise." Again, she wanted to reassure him with her words but she could not deny she felt sick at the thought of what might come out of that woman's mouth.

"I'll leave it up to you then, as long as you prepare yourself. She's out to shock you, to tear us apart, all in the name of revenge." Frank's voice had started to rise even though he had not meant it to.

"I've handled a lot worse, remember? Kick in the gut, hair-pulling, knife in my side? This will only be words, nothing more." Autum was trying to make light of the situation but only she was seeing the funny side of it.

"Be careful. We will discuss it when you come home."

"See you then." She blew him a kiss down the phone before he hung up. She knew what she was going to say.

Hi Isobelle, thanks for the invite, I suppose a drink would be fine. We can meet at Ruby's wine bar next Monday at seven, see you then.

Autum

When Autum arrived home that night, Frank was not in his study, which was very unusual. She made herself a quick snack before heading upstairs. There she found Frank asleep, so she had a shower and slipped into bed as quietly as possible. Once she pulled the covers over herself, she felt Frank stir.

"Hi baby," said Autum as she turned towards him.

"Hi yourself, sexy," replied Frank.

"Is everything OK?" she asked, a bit concerned.

"Yes, just had a really bad headache. Think I have been working myself too hard lately, that's all." He snuggled up to his wife.

"I'll let you sleep then," she whispered by his ear, knowing he had no intention of sleeping now.

"So are you going to meet her?" he asked as he sat up.

"Yes. I have arranged for us to meet up at Ruby's at seven on Monday. So how was your day?" Autum wanted to change the subject quickly so Isobelle did not take over Frank's thoughts. He already had a headache and she wanted to make sure he did not end up with a migraine.

Autum wrapped her arm around his waist and looked up at him, as Frank ran his hand through her hair.

"What you need is to release some of that stress." She moved her hand in between his legs, making him jump just a little.

"You may be right, I have been quite stressed lately." A smile formed on his face and he parted his legs a little more, making himself more comfortable.

Autum slowly grabbed one side of his pyjama pants and started to pull it down as Frank lifted himself up, so that he could pull the other side down. Once that was done, his cock sprang free.

"The doctor did say that keeping certain body parts warm would do wonders for my wellbeing." And with that, he looked down towards "Frank Junior" and gave a little chuckle.

"You mean like this?" Autum slid down and guided his cock into her warm mouth slowly and started to suck, she loved how it always thrilled her to taste him.

"Just like that," was his reply as he watched his wife's head moving up and down. He found that he was slightly lifting up his hips to give her more. When he embedded his hand in her hair, helping her feed off him, well, it only helped spike up his sex drive and still he wanted her to take him deeper.

"Take me deeper," he said, as he felt her stop and look up at him.

Autum repositioned herself so that she was now in between his legs. Her tongue started to lick up from his balls which she had cupped in her hand. She grazed his skin with her teeth, all the way up to the tip, then circled the tip with her tongue over and over again. She looked up to see Frank watching her and smiled. Before Frank knew what hit him, she took him right to the back of her throat, making him gasp out with pleasure. His body felt everything, from the sucking sound she made to the pulling force she was using, and his veins felt like they were stretching out of control. He loved how his hand took control of her hair and guided her up and down. He loved slightly pushing his cock deeper into her mouth, only to hear her moan. She was moving faster now and Frank already knew he couldn't hold out much longer. He raised his hips again to keep up with her rhythm. He felt the build-up to his climax surging through his body, like a dam bursting its banks. "Oh shit," he said, feeling his seed explode through his body into her mouth over and over again. He saw how her cheeks sucked in as she swallowed as her hand worked him for more, draining everything his cock was giving and still he couldn't stop pumping into her mouth. His breathing started to come back to normal and he felt the cold air hit him and the slap of his cock hitting the side of his thigh, as she removed her mouth.

"Has that helped you de-stress?" she asked, sitting up beside her husband.

"Fuck, yes," was his reply. They gave each other a kiss, curled up in bed and fell asleep.

As Autum slept, Frank's mind kept replaying what she had done to him. The more he tried to sleep, the more he dreamt of that sexy mouth around his cock, sucking, pulling and licking it. His cock was obviously enjoying the memory too, as he felt himself getting aroused. He checked his watch and it was four-thirty-seven in the morning but he was now too horny to sleep. He put his arm around his wife and when she cuddled back into him and her ass touched his cock, he knew he had to take her there and then. He rolled her on to her back and he heard a low groan escape her mouth. He ran his hand over her breast and gently squeezed her nipple, rubbing just the tip of it with his fingers until he could feel it getting hard, She was slightly moving in the bed now, as he moved his hand further down her body and in between her legs. He felt her legs trap his hand when he touched her clit but that didn't stop him, it only made it more fun. As he rubbed her clit up and down, she began to moan even more.

"Frank…" She whispered his name without opening her eyes.

"Shush, relax and let me do the work." As he kissed her, he felt her legs fall apart. He continued his onslaught on her clit when he felt her getting wet, he was even more turned on when she inserted *her* fingers inside as he moved his hand out the way, *I love my new dirty wife* he thought to himself.

"Wider, baby," was all Frank said and she spread her legs even more for him. Frank removed the covers from them and placed himself between her legs as she removed her fingers. She grabbed the sheets and arched her back when she felt his tongue suck her. Then he flicked the tip of it with his tongue, as fast as it would go. Frank then inserted his fingers and watched how she pushed herself downwards to fuck them, she placed her finger on her clit and was working it at an alarming speed, she wanted to come but he was not ready for her to come. He wanted her to come around his cock deep inside her. He pulled out his fingers quickly and climbed higher on the bed pulling her negligée up and over her head. He meant it to be graceful but her head fell down with a plonk and she opened her eyes. He apologised.

"Need to fuck you now," he said, as he plunged his tongue deep into her mouth and guided his cock to her opening. He played around her entrance for a bit, enjoying how wet she was and how easily he was going to enter her. He couldn't comprehend how hard he was getting, to the point it was hurting him. He felt her hand on his ass, telling him she was ready, and without another thought, he went straight in, like warriors trying to break down a castle gate with a tree trunk. He cried out as his balls slapped her. He lifted her legs and bent forward and she cried out with the depth of it all. He loved fucking his wife but tonight it seemed like he was an animal, a man possessed. It was like he had not had sex in a long time even though technically he hadn't, he just couldn't get enough. He started to sweat and could feel the sheen of sweat on her body. The smell of sex in the air was intoxicating. It drove his desire more. He loved seeing her breasts bounce with the way he was fucking her and how she was catching her breath, sleep all but forgotten. He turned her over and continued fucking her from behind, spreading her and rubbing her clit and going as deep as he could possibly go.

"Frank, I'm…" was all she could utter as Frank gave her a few more heavy thrusts that sent her over the edge. He held her hips tight so she would not collapse as he continued his pace. Then he nearly lost his balance as his seed shot through him at an incredible speed. He could feel the mixture of heat from the two of them inside her.

"Jesus!" was all he could say, as he pulled out and huddled beside his wife, both panting like mad, unable to keep up with the way their hearts were beating.

"Are you trying to kill me, Frank?" asked Autum.

"I don't know why I feel so horny; I just couldn't keep my hands off you. Are you OK?" he said, turning her to face him.

"Frank, you are always horny but you seem even hornier than normal, if that's possible." She kissed him and laughed out loud.

"I just love you so much, Autum. All I have to do is think of that dripping pussy of yours and I go weak."

"Frank, that mouth of yours!" As she tried to slap him.

"And that pussy of yours! always wet for me" as he grabbed her hands and climbed on top of her, holding both her hands firmly in place above her head and kissing her hard on the mouth.

"You need help!" she said, as he let her go, leaving the bed to grab a quick shower to clean up.

"How am I going to get my eight hours' sleep with someone like you?" she shouted through the bathroom door.

"You're not!" was Frank's reply as he too got out of the bed and headed towards the bathroom.

"Frank!" was all you could hear before the giggles and laughter took over. Autum was dreading how her hair and body would feel in the morning or, should she say, in the next few hours but, right then, she didn't care. It had been so, so worth it.

Chapter Fifteen

Isobelle had a few days to prepare for her meeting with Autum. Although she had sent the email out of a desire for more revenge, she wasn't sure if she could continue ripping their marriage apart. She had seen Frank around the building and out at lunch and he always seemed to be in a good mood. She wondered whether he had said anything to his wife or if he did not remember anything.

Isobelle was shocked on Friday morning when she was called into her boss's office. Her legs were weak and she was feeling a little sick because she could not think why Mrs Lorenzo might want to have a word. She scanned her face to see if she needed to be worried but the woman gave nothing away.

"Please take a seat, Isobelle," said Mrs Lorenzo, smiling pleasantly.

"Is something wrong Mrs Lorenzo?" Isobelle nearly stuttered. *How pathetic do I sound?*

"Of course not! I can bring my employees into my office without it being a telling off, you know." She let out a little chuckle.

Isobelle found herself relaxing a bit more. It didn't seem like she was going to be disciplined and anything else would seem like a bonus. *A bonus?* Maybe that was why she had been called in. After all, Frank did say that she was singing her praises. Isobelle was lost in her thoughts when Mrs Lorenzo began talking and she snapped out of her daydream about how she would spend the money.

"Isobelle, you have been working very hard these last few months and it has not gone un-noticed. I was praising you only the other day to Mr Howard and explaining how I would like you to progress within the department."

"Progress?" The word shot out of her mouth before she could stop herself. Shock, excitement and disbelief all entered her mind.

"Yes, progress. There is a company that we have been looking at for some time that are in trouble. This would be an ideal time to go in there with a proposal. I would like you to attend, along with James, who will be in charge of finance, and Lucy, from marketing. I have arranged for you all to meet up after lunch and spend some time going through what your roles will be. You will need to work together to pull this deal off. I have every faith in you and I know you won't let me down."

Isobelle felt Mrs Lorenzo's stare bore through her as she waited for an answer. Her heart had quickened and her breathing went up a notch.

"Of course I won't let you down, Mrs Lorenzo. It would be nice to work with James and Lucy. I've heard a lot about them."

"And they of you," she replied.

"Oh." Isobelle hoped it was all good things but she kind of doubted it.

"Good. I will get all of your tickets and your hotel sorted out by this afternoon. You leave on Monday to Wales for three days."

"Monday? But that's…" Isobelle stood up, shocked.

"Do you have somewhere better to be?" There was challenge in Mrs Lorenzo's voice.

"No, I don't, it's just the short notice of it all, nothing more." She gave Mrs Lorenzo her best forced smile. Then she turned her back and walked out of her office, mad as hell.

Monday! Why this bloody Monday, of all the days? She flung herself into her chair. *Did Frank plan this? He must have, the coward. I've a good mind to…*

"Is everything alright, Isobelle? You did not seem happy when you were leaving my office. I could tell." Mrs Lorenzo was staring right into Isobelle's face.

"Err, yes, Mrs Lorenzo. Sorry if you thought otherwise! Just was shocked I've been given such a good opportunity, that's all. Thanks again for asking me." She hadn't even seen the woman approach her desk.

She hoped that she had kept her game face on and by the look of Mrs Lorenzo as she left, her lie seemed to have worked. *Monday.* She thought about what she was going to say to Autum about having to rearrange their meeting. Mrs Lorenzo had not only arranged for her to meet up with James and Lucy but she had also got the caterers to prepare a light lunch, which meant she was going nowhere soon. She sighed and decided there was nothing more she could do but get her head down and work. As the hours slipped by, she even found that she was actually enjoying herself with the others. It was five-thirty when they called it a day. She realised that she would have missed Autum but knew that the chances that Frank would still be working were high. She said her goodbyes to James and Lucy and they arranged what time they were meeting at the train station on Monday morning. Then she headed back to her desk. She tapped at her keyboard, played with her pen and just stared at the screen for ages. Eventually, she decided to pick up the phone and call Frank.

"Frank, it's Isobelle."

"I know who it is." Frank had to hit the mute button for a second to calm himself down. Act normal, he tried to tell himself. He was only just controlling himself and she had only said a few words.

"I was trying to get hold of Autum before she left for the day but I was stuck in a meeting and missed her so I thought…"

"You thought that I would pass on the message. Just say what you need to say and I will make sure that she gets it." Again, Frank found it hard to even keep his voice even.

"Can you let her know that I will not be able to make it on Monday as I will be working away with the team and will not be back for a couple of days, as I'm sure you already know."

"I know Mrs Lorenzo was organising for some of her staff to go to Wales but I didn't know who she had decided to send. That is her decision to make. I will let Autum know you cannot make it. Was there anything else?" Frank felt quite smug now. He even felt it in his voice.

"Yes, there is, Frank. Don't play with fire unless you are prepared to get burned." And with that, Isobelle hung up the phone.

"How dare he speak to me like that?" she asked herself aloud, fuming at the smugness in Frank's voice. "He must be forgetting that he's not dealing with Jack anymore. Jack had someone he did not want to lose but I have no one so I have nothing to lose." She screamed out the last few words, happy that her floor was empty. She wanted to throw all her things off her desk like a spoilt, little child but knew she couldn't, so she just grabbed her bag and headed for the one place that she shouldn't have: Frank's office.

"Ignorant bitch!" thought Frank, when she hung up on him. He had promised he would not rise to what she had done but he was struggling. *Don't play with fire? She's the one who's playing with fire, if she thinks I am just going to put up with her and her mind games...* He was packing up ready to leave when his phone rang; it was Autum.

"Hi honey, what's up?" Frank was glad of the distraction.

"Nothing much, the trains have been delayed so I wanted to know if you wanted to meet up in the West End later and grab a bite to eat?"

"That would be a great idea. Just what I need at the moment."

"That bad, huh?"

"You have no idea," Frank began but before he could say anything else, his door burst open to a screaming, mad woman.

"Who the hell do you think you are, Frank?" shouted Isobelle.

"How dare you burst into my office," Frank responded.

"Frank… is that Isobelle? Frank?" Autum was trying her best to listen.

"Do you think you are dealing with Jack? Do you?" Isobelle stormed towards his desk.

"Autum, I have to go…"

"Don't hang up on me, Frank. Don't do anything stupid. Promise me. She's not worth it," said Autum, squeezing out as much as she could in one breath.

"I love you," he said and he hung up the phone.

She needed to be home, she needed air and she needed to make sure that Frank was OK. She redialled his number again and again and again as tears started to roll down her cheeks. She knew she didn't look good, didn't care who was sitting beside her, only that Frank was in trouble. She dialled again but this time she rang reception and informed security that an employee had broken into Frank's office, was verbally abusing him and needed to be removed instantly. There was nothing more she could do besides wait for Frank to call her back; it was going to be the longest wait of her life.

Frank moved from around the back of his desk and came face to face with Isobelle who had grabbed hold of his letter opener.

"Do you think I am afraid of you?" spat Isobelle, poking him in the chest with it.

Frank could not contain his anger any longer. Without thinking, he grabbed her by the throat, pushing her backwards towards his door.

"How dare you come in here, shouting like that? How dare you threaten me with your cheap shots, thinking to actually do me harm with that?" His grip on her throat tightened.

"Frank, you're hurting me," she said, trying to get out of his grip on her throat dropping the opener by her feet.

"Stay away from me and Autum, otherwise the only person getting burned will be you." Frank looked her straight in the eye without blinking before he let her go.

Isobelle caught her breath and rubbed her throat.

"Get out of my office," said Frank, turning his back and walking to his desk.

"You bastard," was all Isobelle said as she charged at him the weapon back in her hand. But before she could make contact with Frank, she felt a strong hand gripping her waist and realised her legs were now dangling in the air. She had been about to stab Frank in the back when security had grabbed her.

"Mr Howard, are you OK?" Bob asked him.

"I'm fine, Bob. Just get her out of here and make sure that she doesn't come back."

"Yes, sir," he said as he led her away kicking and screaming.

"She's dead, Frank. An eye for an eye!" Isobelle managed to shout, before Bob spun her around and pinned both of her hands behind her back.

"You're hurting me," Frank heard her say faintly as she was led down the hall. Then all he could hear was his own breathing. He remained still for what seemed like ages before Bob interrupted his thoughts. He didn't even hear him enter.

"I have revoked her access and have made the changeover guard aware of the situation, sir."

"Thank you, Bob," said Frank.

"It's your wife you need to thank, sir. She made the call. Do you need me to escort you to your car, sir?"

"My wife?" Frank's mind was a mess and he couldn't understand how Autum had spoken to Bob until he remembered that she had been speaking to him when Isobelle burst in. He quickly pulled out his phone and saw all the missed calls from his wife.

"Mr Howard?" said Bob.

"Oh, sorry, Bob. No, I'll be OK. Thanks again." He dialled his wife's number.

"Frank, oh God, you're alive!" said Autum, starting to cry.

"Don't cry baby, I'm fine. Just come home." Frank had no energy to speak.

"Are you hurt? What did she want?" Autum asked.

"Just come home to me."

"Did you see Bob?"

"Yes, I did and thank you."

"For what?" Autum asked.

"For Bob. he saved my life," said Frank, trying to laugh off the insane situation.

"My God, Frank, what the hell did she do?"

"I'll tell you when you get back. Just let me know when your train is due in and I will pick you up."

"OK," she said and reluctantly put down the phone.

With the train slightly delayed, Autum got back to London just after eight. She didn't think she had ever been so glad to get off a train. She ran out of the station and headed to where Frank usually parked to meet her.

"Oh God, Frank," she said, flinging her arms around him and nearly kissing him to death.

Frank enjoyed the embrace of his wife and the demand of her kiss.

"Are you alright? What happened? Why was she there?"

Frank laughed, wrapped his arm around his wife's waist, guided her inside the car and drove home. He told her everything that had happened, except the part when Isobelle had said that she was going to kill Autum.

Chapter Sixteen

Isobelle couldn't believe what was happening to her as she was lead out of the building, by Bob of all people, kicking and screaming. What the hell had come over her, she did not know. She had been mad, that much was obvious, but she couldn't believe she had done something *that* stupid. She tried to kill him, she was willing to kill Frank out of anger. The evening air hit her.

"I need to get my stuff from the office," she said in between pants.

"Not going to happen," said Bob.

"My coat and stuff – what will happen to them?"

"You wait outside and I will bring them to you. Give me your pass and keys." Bob held out his hand.

"I didn't mean to upset Frank…" She was cut off before she could continue.

"I think you mean 'Mr Howard'". Bob gave her a look that said, "Don't test me, because I will hurt you."

"Bob, if you speak to *Mr Howard,* he will confirm we just had a slight disagreement."

"Is that before or after you tried to attack him with a weapon?"

"I was only trying to get his attention!" she knew that sounded even worse.

"Save it. I'm not interested. Just give me your pass and keys."

"How the hell did you know I was there?" Isobelle tried to think back to what had happened. Had he seen her on the cameras maybe? She didn't think that Frank had a panic button. Or did he? She would never know. She thought about how he had moved when she had burst into his office. He was on the phone with one hand on his desk, so he couldn't have pressed anything unless… *Autum. That bitch must have heard me when I entered and called Bob.* She laughed inwardly to herself. *Always one step ahead…*

"I'm waiting. Don't let me ask you again." Bob's voice was full of warning.

"Fine." She slammed her hand into her bag and pulled out her pass and keys. She stopped for a brief second to look at the building in which she had worked for several years. One stupid action had resulted in her losing the job she loved. *Well, maybe not one…* There was only one person she blamed and it was not herself. Once again, she had nothing but hate and revenge to keep her company. *You're so going to pay, Autum, and you can give my regards to Jack when you see him.* She was interrupted by Bob.

"Pass and keys!" he shouted. "Now!"

"Here," was all she said as she threw them at him, just missing his face.

The look Isobelle received meant to kill her but she didn't care. Bob turned his back towards her and headed back into the building. Once he was inside, he turned to face her and smiled, waving her pass and keys.

"Bastard!" she shouted, then paced up and down outside the building, waiting for her belongings to be brought down.

Ten minutes passed before Bob returned with a small box and her coat over his arm. As he came out of the building, Isobelle headed towards him.

"Thanks," she said, as she held out her hands. She was calmer now. But Bob didn't acknowledge her, just handed over the box, gave her the coat and headed back into the building. Isobelle put on her coat and looked into the box: a few personal items and her diary. That's all she had to show for herself. She placed the box under her arm and headed home.

She was used to the silence that greeted her now. She placed the box down in the living room. As she sat down, she took a good look around the place and realised there was nothing left for her there. *Maybe this is the best thing that could have happened.* She would always seem worthless to everyone else but maybe she just needed a break for a while. She could come back and then decide what she was going to do. *What a fucking day.* She picked up her diary and flicked over a few pages, looking at what she had done over the past months: meetings with her boss, workshops she had attended, times she had spoken to Autum about Jack. The notes about Autum and Jack got more and more disturbing as she flicked through. "All Jack talks about is Autum. She needs to be gone." And, "Rebecca thinks she's special, I will show her how special she really is." On some pages were just single words or phrases, like "KILL", "Hurt" and "No more pain". She closed the diary. All she wanted was the pain to just go away. Isobelle entered the kitchen, poured herself a drink and turned on the radio to relax herself. Then she headed into the bedroom and looked at the bed. Only half of it would ever be occupied again. She put down her glass, stepped into a wardrobe and started to sniff Jack's clothes. She was clinging on to him, a man that had never really loved her but, in his own strange way, had cared for her. The man that she had been so happy with. Because of that, despite everything, she still couldn't hate him. He had made her feel so alive, he had defended her when Autum had thrown her lunch at her and slapped her in the face. *All he ever wanted to see was that me and Autum had made peace. Peace…* Isobelle rubbed at her temple. She felt like her head had been overloaded with pressure and wanted to explode. She wanted for all the pain to go away but didn't know how that could happen. Jack was the love of her life, although their relationship had been short-lived. As she remembered him, tears flowed down her cheeks. She sniffed his clothes again and noted that his scent was nearly gone. She knew that when there was nothing left of him to smell, she would lose him forever. That thought made her tears flow more freely so that she was sobbing. She headed towards the bed and curled up with her pillow for comfort like a baby.

Isobelle heard a bleeping noise and jumped up. It was seven-fifteen. She turned off her alarm and, without thinking, headed for the bathroom for a shower. As she passed the living room, she heard the radio, which meant it had been on all night. She needed to pop into work to finish off some paperwork but as she hit the shower, she remembered the events of the night before. There would be no going into work, not today, not ever. After she had dressed, she made a quick breakfast and then decide what she wanted to do going forward. The only way she could do that was by paying a visit to Jack's grave. She was hoping that she could find some answers there. When she approached the grave, she noticed a dozen white roses that seemed to light up the scene. Her movements quickened. She wanted to find out who had placed them there. She could think of only one person it could have been. She looked at the small tag dangling from the stem.

Forever in my thoughts. Sorry I did not tell you enough how proud I was of you. Love you, son. Jason

Jason must have had someone deliver them, she thought as she removed all of the old flowers and tidied up the area, talking to Jack as she went along.

"Hi Jack. So much has happened since I last came to visit you. Your dad stayed for a bit but has gone back home now. He has found someone to take over the company now you're not here. I miss you so much, Jack. I seem to be getting myself into more and more trouble with Autum and now I have been fired from my job by attacking Frank." She talked for ages, telling Jack that Frank and Autum were plotting against her and that she could not manage by herself. She asked Jack to give her the strength to continue.

She had brought a single rainbow flower which she thought suited Jack's personality, *forever changing.* She placed it in the middle of his grave.

"Thank you, Jack," was all she said before blowing a kiss and leaving. Isobelle felt like a weight had been lifted off her shoulders. She knew that she could not let Jack's death be in vain but she also knew that she had no strength to continue by herself anymore. When she returned home, she thought about the card that Jason had left. *Will he be happy to see me?* He had left without saying goodbye but then she knew that he was probably ashamed of what they had both done. She wasn't though. Maybe it was inappropriate but, all the same, he had been good for an older man. It was then that she decided what she wanted to do. Her mobile started to ring, which made her jump because she could not think who it could be. She did not recognise the number. She thought about cancelling the call but decided out of curiosity to take it.

"Hello?" she said.

"Am I speaking to Isobelle?"

"Who's calling?" was her reply.

"Isobelle, this is Mrs Lorenzo. Do you have a minute?"

Isobelle was lost for words. Why did she want to speak to her on a Saturday morning? Did she also want to have a go at her for what she did to Frank? Did she want to give her two pennies' worth as well? Might as well find out, thought Isobelle, taking a deep breath and putting on her professional voice.

"Hello, Mrs Lorenzo. I wasn't expecting a call from you. How can I help you?" She prepared herself for the answer.

"Mr Howard called me late last night and informed me of what happened..." Isobelle cut her off mid flow:

"I don't know what came over me. If I could take back what I did, I would. I never meant to upset him." She needed to keep calm and control her temper.

"I'm not sure what you did that caused him to fire you but you really were essential to this project. Usually, I would not intercept a decision of Mr Howard's but I need this project to go well."

Isobelle was trying to digest what Mrs Lorenzo was saying. There was no way she could have got her job back. Or could she?

"Mrs Lorenzo, I'm not sure what you are trying to say?" Isobelle did not want to build up her hopes; there was no way Frank would give her her job back.

"We have come to an agreement."

"Agreement?" Isobelle did not mean to butt in.

"Yes," Mrs Lorenzo replied, "you have been given a chance to redeem yourself. Do well on this project and secure this deal and you will be allowed to return to work."

Isobelle still couldn't believe she would get her job back. What was he playing at? Why would he do this for her? He owed her nothing, which meant there must be a catch.

"What's the catch?" It came out hard-hitting and blunt, not how she had meant to say it.

"Do well, Isobelle, and prove to me that it was worth putting up a fight for you." And with that, Mrs Lorenzo hung up the phone.

Isobelle wanted to jump up and down with excitement but that doubt just kept creeping back into her mind: why would he do this? She put it to one side and refocused her mind. She had it in her to win this deal. Being around Autum over the years, she had learned a lot and listened to how Autum worked, how she put her case across to get them to sign on the dotted line. That was one thing she couldn't take away from Autum. She was brilliant at what she did and deserved to be praised and to have been promoted to her new position. Nevertheless, Isobelle found it unnerving thinking about her *in a good way.*

The rest of the weekend flew by and all Isobelle could focus on was the end prize: getting her job back, the one she loved so much. When she met up with James and Lucy at the train station on Monday, she greeted both of them with a smile. The journey would take them just over three hours so it would be a good chance to really get to know them. They sat down and began to talk as the train departed.

Chapter Seventeen

Frank had had a stressful night's sleep but he needed to keep level-headed. Once again, he needed to keep his wife safe, so he rang his contacts to put things in place. He knew he would have to broach the subject but not just yet. He would try and slip it into a conversation over dinner or in bed. The thought of the latter made him smile. He also wanted to track Isobelle's whereabouts so he was going to hire a detective to follow her. That would make him feel better, knowing he knew where she was, but he had so much going on in his mind that he forgot to put that action in place.

He remembered that he needed to ring Mrs Lorenzo to update her on what he had done and explain that Isobelle would not be working for the company anymore. It was Saturday morning but Frank was always in work-mode, especially when in his study.

"Mrs Lorenzo, it's Frank. Sorry to ring you on the weekend but I need to inform you of some events that happened yesterday."

"Sophia. No need to be so formal, Frank."

"Sorry, Sophia, but it's about one of your employees: Isobelle."

"What about her?"

"I had to let her go yesterday. She burst into my office and tried to attack me because she did not like the tone of my voice when she was passing me a message to give to my wife. "

"Frank, I need her to help James and Lucy with this company in Wales. She's good. You sure you didn't just overreact?"

Frank felt his blood rising but he did not want Sophia to know the depth of what had been going on.

"She overstepped the mark. Security had to be called in to remove her. I do not want her back."

"Whatever went on, I'm sure she is regretting it now." Sophia was trying to appeal to Frank's softer side but it wasn't working so she tried something else.

"I will take full responsibility." She could tell he was considering it because she could hear his heavy breathing.

"Fine but there are two conditions. If she fails to secure this company, then she's gone. If, however, the trip proves to be a success then… I may consider her return, on the understanding that her access to certain parts of the building would be blocked. Understood?" What the hell had he just agreed to?

"Understood," was Sophia's reply. They talked for a while longer, before Frank said his goodbyes.

Bloody women, he thought to himself, they always find a way to turn something around. *Was I overreacting? Like hell I was. And now I have agreed to take that psycho back at work.* All of his plans now seemed up in the air. He was thinking about how he

170

was going to keep an eye on that mad bitch but he was more concerned about how to bring up the subject with his wife. He thought about taking her out for dinner and telling her then. The chances of them getting through it without arguing would be next to none. And the chances of having sex would probably be zero. *Great!*

He took a break from work as it was now lunchtime. He had made a reservation at a restaurant that evening for four: himself, Autum, Rebecca and Julian. It should be a good chance for them all to relax and have fun. Rosetta had prepared a light lunch for them both. Frank told her not to cook any dinner as they were going to eat out. Rosetta started to babble on in a mixture of Spanish and English that she felt like her food was not good enough, which they both knew was absurd. Frank grabbed her and kissed her on the cheek, laughing, as he knew this would send her Spanish into overdrive, which indeed it did. Autum came in not long after; she had popped out to get some new work clothes.

"What's so funny?" she asked him.

"Oh, I told Rosetta that we are going out for dinner," he said, still chuckling to himself.

"Ah," was all Autum could say, as she knew how defensive Rosetta was about her cooking.

"We're eating out?" she enquired.

"Yes, I have reserved a table for four as I've invited Rebecca and Julian," Frank said with a smile.

"Thanks, that's a nice gesture. Are we celebrating something?" Autum looked directly at her husband to see if she could spot any clues.

"Can't a man take his wife and friends out to dinner?" Frank was no good at this. He decided it would be better (he hoped) if he just told Autum what was going on now. She would find out eventually somehow. If he told her now she would have several hours to calm down; if he told her later then he would end up sleeping in one of the spare rooms.

"Frank, I know that look. You're hiding something." Autum put her hands on her hips.

"OK, something happened this morning when you left."

"I knew it. What has she done now?"

"It's not like that," Frank said, too softly.

"What have you done?" Autum raised her voice.

"You know Mrs Lorenzo? Sophia, I should say. From work…" Frank didn't finish.

"You've given her her job back, haven't you?"

"Sophia said she would take full responsibility." Again he was cut off.

"How could you, Frank? Who owns this company, you or Sophia?" Autum started to walk out of the kitchen.

"I have put some conditions into the agreement," he said, trailing after his wife.

"I thought this was sorted!" she said, continuing to climb the stairs.

"It was. It is. I promise you. I will be blocking her access to certain floors." Frank was climbing the stairs two at a time to keep up with her.

"Like that's gonna stop her!" She started to take out the things she had bought and force them into her wardrobe.

Frank tried to wrap his arms around his wife but she pulled away.

"Don't think you can get around me that easily."

172

"She won't hurt us, I promise." Again, he tested the waters and tried to hug her and this time she did not push him away.

"When will this end?" she asked, looking into Frank's eyes as he pulled her close.

The rest of the afternoon went by quietly. Frank knew Autum was still upset with him so he decided to keep his distance and stay in his study. Autum said she was going out and Frank presumed that she would be popping over to Rebecca's house; this gave him time to consider whether he really had done the right thing.

Autum had phoned Rebecca en route to say that she needed a chat and was on her way. When she arrived at Rebecca's, she just broke down.

"What's happened?" said Rebecca, bringing her into the apartment.

"Isobelle attacked Frank on Friday."

"What? Is he OK?" Rebecca replied, as she sat next to Autum on the sofa.

"He wouldn't have been if I had not heard part of the conversation and rung Bob to get that woman removed from the building," Autum replied, feeling more at ease.

Autum told Rebecca everything that Frank had told her.

"So what you're saying is that he sacked her and then re-employed her the next day?"

"Yep," was all Autum could say.

Rebecca wanted to change the subject and started to talk about the dinner planned that night.

"Julian is really looking forward to some man talk," she said, starting to laugh.

"I think Frank is as well."

"Fancy a latte?" said Rebecca, getting up and heading towards the kitchen.

"Love one."

"Have you eaten lunch yet?" Rebecca asked with raised eyebrows.

"I'm not hungry," Autum replied.

"Give me twenty minutes and I will whip something up and I won't take no for an answer. You're looking pale, girl." She meant it as a joke but she did notice how ill-looking Autum was becoming.

Autum laughed.

"You're always trying to fatten me up, that's your problem."

"Well someone has to." They continued chatting and having banter for nearly two hours.

It was soon time for Autum to leave and she felt ten times better for having come there. She thanked Rebecca for the lunch and said, "See you later," as she headed out of the door. When she arrived home, she headed towards the study to see if Frank was still working.

"Hi," she said, popping her head round the door.

Frank got up and walked towards her.

"You OK?" He kissed her lightly.

"I'm fine, just going to lie down for a bit, if that's OK?"

"OK, will check on you later." He kissed her again and watched her head upstairs.

As Frank sat back down, he wondered if everything that was happening was getting too much for Autum. He had never seen her take a nap before and she was looking off-colour. He would check on her later and if she still didn't look up to it, he would cancel

174

dinner. Just after four, he brought her up a hot chocolate. She was still fast asleep, so he sat on the bed and woke her.

"Brought you up a hot drink," he said, as she began to stir.

Autum sat up and took the hot drink, which was covered in cream and marshmallows.

"Why is everyone trying to fatten me up? First Rebecca and now you!" She took a sip of the drink, a dollop of cream and a mouthful of marshmallows.

"I can take it away if you want," he said, watching how much she was enjoying it.

"Try it," she joked, a smile lighting up her face.

"Autum, are you OK? I've never seen you have a nap in the afternoon before and you are looking a bit pale. Do you think you are coming down with some type of bug?"

"Not that I know of. I don't feel sick. You must have been speaking to Rebecca as she said the same thing earlier." She looked up to see his reaction.

"Not guilty. But if she also thinks that, then she must be worried." He was hoping that she would just go to the doctors to get them off her back.

"I know that look, Frank. I'm fine. I don't need to see a doctor. I've just had a lot on my mind, that's all."

"I'm sorry if I am the cause of this. I didn't mean to make you ill."

"For the umpteenth time, I am not ill, just tired." She gulped down another mouthful of cream and marshmallows.

"Do you still want to go out for dinner? I can cancel it if you…" Autum cut him off.

"Don't you dare cancel. I am looking forward to dinner and so is Rebecca and I know you could do with catching up with Julian for some man talk."

Frank laughed and got off the bed.

"I'll leave you to rest," he said and headed back downstairs.

When Autum had finished her drink, she got out of bed and headed towards the bathroom to look at herself. As she did so, she realised for the first time that she did look a bit off-colour. *How come I never spotted this before?* She ran her hand over her face and noticed how tired she looked but it didn't take her long to dismiss it. Autum felt she had just convinced herself she did not look well because people around her were telling her she did not look well. After her shower, she felt a new burst of energy. Her hair had been set in rollers for later and her outfit had been picked and was hanging on the outside of her wardrobe.

Frank came back upstairs after thirty minutes to see if his wife had fallen back asleep and was surprised to find she was up, had had a shower and had set her hair in rollers. Autum got up and walked over to Frank in her robe.

"See. I don't look pale." She crossed her arms.

"Well, let's see." He opened up her arms and slowly loosened her robe.

"I thought it was my face," she said, her eyes following his hands.

"I just said that you're looking a bit pale and it's best if I check you over, just to make sure." He opened up her robe and took in her nakedness.

Autum's skin prickled as she felt her robe slipping from her shoulders.

"Naked with curlers…" he said, as he pulled her to him and kissed her hard.

Autum opened her mouth for him and his tongue took over tasting chocolate and mashmellows on her tongue; she wrapped her hands around him and pulled him deeper into her totally addicted to his scent and his body. He broke away to tear away at his clothes before capturing her mouth again. He carried her to the bed and laid her down but her rollers dug into her.

"Frank, my hair!" she said, giggling as she touched it.

"Fuck the hair," he replied, taking her nipple into his mouth and pulling at it with his teeth.

She arched her back as he let go, then felt the heat of his breath against her ear. The grazing of his lips against her skin made her heart beat quicker, as she grabbed his hair.

"Frank," she whispered, feeling his cock press into her stomach.

"Whatever you want, baby, just tell me." His tongue slid down her neck as he suck on her tender flesh.

"Promise me you'll always be there."

Frank lifted himself up to look at his wife. It was a strange thing to say. She knew he would move heaven and earth to protect her: she was his life, his love and his being.

"Always." He lowered himself back down, guided his cock to her entrance and thrust himself in.

"Always," he repeated as he continued his onslaught on her body. He could feel her insides sucking him deeper and closing around him. He rolled over so that she could straddle him. He loved to watch her body move, see the look on her face as she tilted her head back, and feel how her hips gyrated over him as he reached up to massage her breasts, soft moans escaping those beautiful lips making him swell even more. He grabbed hold of her hips and worked with her body to meet his thrusts whilst lifting up his own. He was sweating and she was panting as he brought her down to kiss him. He moved his hands to grab her ass and work its movement. He squeezed and pulled it and she reached behind her and cupped his balls, making him moan into her mouth. He moved one hand so that his fingers could rub across her clit. Autum broke away from the kiss, leaving pleasurable noises behind. She was now upright again and working her hips. It was getting too much for her, he was rock hard inside her, his fingers were punishing her clit and her mind was in meltdown.

Frank could feel her coming; he could feel the movement building up inside her.

"Look at me when you come," was all he said as she fought hard to stay focused. He put more pressure on her hips as he picked up the pace, quicker and harder, until she finally gave in and screamed out.

"I love you," was all he could muster as he let loose his own climax, continuing to pump and she continuing to grind until they both finally stopped and she collapsed on top of him.

Chapter Eighteen

They met up for dinner, the men sitting next to each other whilst their partners sat opposite.

"You're looking much better," said Rebecca, noticing how much colour Autum had in her cheeks.

"Had a bit of an 'afternoon nap', if you know what I mean…" Autum gave Rebecca a wink.

"Dirty girl!" They both started laughing.

"Not going to share the joke?" asked Julian.

"You really don't want to know," replied Rebecca, as they continued to look through their menus, the girls giggling.

The evening was going well and Frank was glad that he had invited Autum's friends. He was having a great conversation with Julian, trying to introduce him to the world of golf. Julian laughed him off; with the way he was built, golf would make him look like a bodybuilder swinging a lollypop stick. The evening drew on and the meal became a distant memory and at last they decided to call it a night.

"We need to organise another girlie night," said Autum, having had far too much wine.

"Yes, we should," Rebecca replied as she gave Autum a goodbye hug.

"I'll let the girls know then." Frank wrapped her coat around her shoulders and they left the restaurant.

On Sunday, Frank was working early in his study and making calls when Autum disturbed him and told him to come and eat some breakfast. *It's seven in the morning and he's already making calls.* As they talked, Frank's phone rang and Autum thought how rarely Frank had time to relax.

"Hi, Julian, what can I do for you?" said Frank, making his way out of the kitchen to talk shop. By the time he returned twenty minutes later, Autum had left. When he called her, she called back from the living room, so he joined her in there in a joyful mood.

"That was my old friend Julian from Barcelona."

"Barcelona? I thought it was Julian from last night. What did he want? She asked nervously Autum thought back to how Frank had been duped into going there before, only to be met by Jason. She sat up.

Frank sat beside his wife and gave her a kiss.

"He apologised profusely about what happened last time. We all know that Jason was a different man back then. No, this is genuine business and he wants me to fly over for a few days to meet some associates."

"How soon?"

"Not for another three weeks."

"Will you be staying long?" Autum asked.

"Thursday to Saturday," Frank replied.

Autum felt a bit more at ease. She had a few weeks before he left and she would make the most of it.

180

She watched how his face lit up as he talked about the new people he was going to meet and what he could do for them or they for him. It brought her joy.

"You sure you will be alright?" he said, hugging his wife closer.

"Yes, I will be fine." She kissed him.

"What do you want to do today?" Frank enquired.

"Surprise me."

He got up and tapped his phone to his lips.

"Surprise it will be then," he said, walking out and tapping numbers into his phone.

Autum relaxed back on the sofa, thinking of what her surprise could be. She couldn't keep still because she was so excited. She ran upstairs, trying to prepare what she should wear in her head. She laid out outfits on the bed. As Frank entered the room, he started to laugh.

"Which one do you think would suit me best?" Autum had played this game before when he had taken her to the Bahamas and he had given nothing away then.

"You would look lovely in all of them, my dear." Frank loved this game because he always won.

"So I am picking the right outfits then?" Autum felt confident this time around.

"Well, that depends on whether you're going to be indoors or outdoors." You're not going to win, he thought.

"Outdoors?" She had not considered that. She went back into her wardrobe and pulled out some trousers and accessories to match.

"Pick one for each," she challenged him.

"What fun would there be in that?" He turned and walked out of the bedroom. Game, set and match, he thought to himself. He laughed, hearing Autum screeching behind him.

A few hours later and after plenty of nagging from Autum, they left the house. Autum had settled on trousers for the day. The journey took fifty minutes.

"We're by the river," said Autum, as they arrived.

"Yes, we are going on a river cruise."

Autum was so excited; although she lived in London, she had never been on a river cruise. As they approached the boat, she could hear music in the background.

"Jazz," she said happily, as Frank helped her aboard the boat.

The ambience was just amazing. There was a jazz band playing in the background, the table settings were just divine and Autum could not have thought of a better surprise than this.

"Frank, this is just beautiful," she said, kissing him on his cheek.

"Just like my wife," he replied, hugging her, as they were guided to their table.

They didn't even realise the boat had departed until they looked out of the window.

Frank watched in awe as his wife took in the boat. Its structure was entirely made of glass, giving everyone onboard the most magnificent views of London.

The boat was full and everyone was dressed for the occasion. The air was filled with laughter and love. Frank looked around at the other passengers. Some were tourists, others were treating loved ones and some were just doing something out of the ordinary on a Sunday. As the food started to arrive and the drink started to flow, Frank realised it was the best surprise he could have given Autum; everything was just perfect.

"Look, isn't that…" Autum felt like a child being taken on a trip. She was so excited pointing out landmarks that she forgot she was on a boat, surrounded by people.

Frank laughed out loud at his wife's excitement, wishing he had thought of doing this before.

"Yes, that is the Houses of Parliament." He watched lovingly as she ate her food, sang quietly to the old jazz classics and continued pointing out landmark buildings passing by.

Before they knew it, it was time to depart the two and a half hour trip.

"Frank, that was truly amazing. Thank you," said Autum and overpowered his mouth with a kiss.

They spent the next few hours just looking around, holding hands and of course indulging in some retail therapy. They headed back home just after five. Rosetta had already prepared dinner, which was gladly received, since they had had lunch early. After that, they felt so exhausted that they could do nothing more than just relax on the sofa. After an hour or so, Frank headed back to his study to work whilst Autum spent the next twenty-five minutes telling Rebecca about the fabulous day she had just had.

It was seven when she went into the study to see Frank tapping away at his computer.

"Fancy a break?" she asked, seeing Frank rub his eyes.

"Yeah, why not?" he said, moving from behind his desk towards her.

They headed towards the kitchen and made drinks.

"It's been a while since you went away," she said, as she brought her mug to her mouth and hugged the mug for comfort.

Frank turned to look at Autum. He was concerned that she looked worried and he did not know why. They had had the most brilliant day but she now seemed so different. He wondered whether someone had said something.

"Is something bothering you?" he said, taking the mug from her and placing it down. "Has someone said anything?" He turned her head towards him.

"She's out there, isn't she?" Autum felt a chill down her spine.

Frank was so taken aback that he found himself speechless for a second.

"She won't get the chance to come near you. I've seen to that." Frank only realised what he had just admitted after the words left his mouth.

Autum jumped up as if she had been prodded with a hot iron.

"What did you just say?" Fear, shock and confused thoughts came alive and filled her mind.

Fuck, he thought to himself, seeing the anger building up in her face.

"I said you have nothing to worry about." He was now preparing for fireworks.

"Liar! What do you mean she won't get the chance? What the hell are you hiding from me, Frank?" She was almost hyperventilating.

Frank made mistake number two by taking too long to answer her.

"Something else happened in that office, didn't it?" she said, raising her voice.

Frank tried to calm her down. He could see she was really losing it, big-time, and he was scared of what she would do when, or if, he told her the truth.

"Frank!" she screamed as loud as she could at him.

"Calm down, you're scaring me," he said holding her shoulders.

"Tell me," was all she replied, after taking in a heavy breath.

"What I told you was correct. I just didn't think you needed to know anything else. She was speaking in anger." Frank could feel his heart beating almost out of his chest.

"What did she say?" She looked him straight in the eye. She knew she could handle whatever that bitch was going to throw at her. She was stronger now; she had to be.

"She said… she was going to kill you. 'An eye for an eye.'" He bowed his head, unable to look at her.

She hissed in a breath and he felt her shake. Then her body went rigid. He looked at her, unsure whether she was in a state of shock. Whatever was happening to her, he was worried.

"Autum?" She didn't respond.

"Autum!" Frank began to panic. He shook her but she didn't even blink.

He stood up and, zombie-like, she stood up too. He let go of her shoulders and watched her turn towards the door as if she were having some out-of-body experience.

"I'm sorry I didn't tell you. I didn't want you to worry." He found himself crying.

"I would never let anyone hurt you, you know that. Just speak to me, please. I beg you." But Autum just continued walking. When he placed himself in front of her, he saw that she had tears in her eyes and that was what broke him.

"I love you," he said through his tears, kneeling down in front of her and wrapping his arms around her legs.

Autum knew she was in shock. Why she had gone into meltdown, she didn't know. All she knew was that she just couldn't speak. She heard everything Frank had said to her and his reasoning behind what he had done but she still couldn't respond. *The bitch wants to kill me. "An eye for an eye."* It was those words that bore through her soul and that had put her in this state. She felt Frank's pain and tears rolled down her face but it was only when she felt him wrap himself around her legs that she found she could snap out of whatever had tried to drag her down. She put her hand on Frank's head and looked down at him.

Frank couldn't believe what was happening. They had had the most beautiful day out, a fantastic dinner and had spent some quality time in each other's arms. Then something had happened. He still couldn't figure out how that bitch had come up in conversation. She always seemed to know how to ruin a good day, even without being there. He was pissed off at this endless cycle. All he wanted to do was to make Autum happy. Jack had been bad enough and Frank thought that finally, fucking finally, he and Autum could lead a happy life. But oh, no, that psycho-bitch had to take over where Jack left off. Frank was still absorbed in his thoughts when he felt Autum's warm hand touch him. He looked up at her and rose.

"I'm so sorry," he said, hugging her for dear life.

"I'm fine," she said, in a just-about-audible voice.

As Frank let her go, he noticed how pale she had got.

"Autum, you don't look well," he said, an understatement after what had just gone on.

"I'm fine, Frank," said Autum but she knew she wasn't. She felt something else happening to her that she couldn't describe. She started to feel light-headed and the room seemed hazy.

"You don't look it," he said, guiding her into the living room. He suddenly felt all her weight on him. She had passed out.

Frank quickly laid her on the floor and patted her face lightly. He called out her name several times but got no joy, so he pulled out his phone and dialled for an ambulance. Frank felt embarrassed when he was questioned on what had happened. All he said was that his wife had received some shocking news, which was the truth.

When Autum started to wake, the first thing she felt was something over her mouth. She automatically reached for it and began to panic. She could see someone leaning over her but could not focus clearly on who it was. She whispered Frank's name.

"I'm here, honey." He moved the hair that was resting on her face.

"Where am I?" she asked. He grabbed her hand and explained that she was in an ambulance and that she had collapsed.

The medic took over and all Frank could do was hold her hand. Once they arrived at the hospital, she was put in a cubical, while Frank gave the reception all of his wife's details and explained what had happened. Autum had blacked out for quite some time and the doctor wanted to run some tests to make sure that everything was OK and check that there was no underlying cause that had triggered things.

Frank was racked with guilt. "If only," he kept saying to himself over and over again, pacing up and down and waiting for his wife to come back. Then he changed it to, "What if?" His mind was tearing him apart. Finally he heard voices. Autum was wheeled in on a bed and then they were left alone.

Autum still didn't look well; she was still pale. He pulled up the chair and didn't say a word, just reached out and held her hand.

"What did they say?" he finally asked, to fill the silence.

"Not much. They ran a few tests, took some samples and said they would get a doctor to speak to me later," she said, turning to face him.

"Autum, I'm sorry for doing this to you. I…" She cut him off.

"Stop blaming yourself. It could have been worse. I could have been just wearing your shirt with nothing underneath. Now that would have taken some explaining," she said, trying to make light of the situation.

Frank knew what she was trying to do but he found it hard to see the funny side.

"You scared the living daylights out of me back there," he replied.

"I just don't know what happened. I couldn't stop it. I think I must be sick, Frank. I'm scared."

Frank rose from the chair to cuddle his wife's face with his own, as she hugged him, crying.

"I'm here for you, baby. No matter what." He tried to hold back his own tears, wanting to be strong for his wife.

Frank didn't know how long they had been there when a doctor appeared.

"Mrs Howard, I'm Dr Andrew Keen. I have your results back." He turned to face Frank. "You must be Mr Howard." Frank nodded.

"Is everything OK, doctor?" said Frank as he hugged Autum closer.

"Everything seemed fine, nothing out of the ordinary appeared on the scans. Your blood pressure is a little too high, which is understandable under the circumstances. Other than that you are both doing fine."

"What do you mean 'both'?" said Frank and Autum in unison, looking at each other.

"You're pregnant, Mrs Howard. Around nine weeks, give or take. I have written out a prescription for you and I would like you to come back in for a check-up soon. Give this note to reception when you leave so that they can book you in for a visit when you hit twelve weeks." And with that, he tore a piece of paper from his pad and handed it to her.

"We're having a baby," Autum gasped, still almost too shocked for words.

"I'm going to be a father." Frank felt emotional. He lowered his head and kissed his wife.

"Congratulations, Mr and Mrs Howard," said the doctor and left the room.

Chapter Nineteen

Autum and Frank left the hospital still in shock. They hardly said a word but held hands and glanced at each other. Autum heard Frank whisper, "Baby…" and saw him smile, which made her proud. Frank tried to help her into the car but she raised her eyebrows.

"Really?" She crossed her arms over her chest. Frank still held the door open.

"Really," Frank replied and gave his wife a helping hand into the car.

They made the journey back home relatively quickly and headed towards the sofas.

"Frank, about earlier…" Autum tried to continue.

"Don't. Please, not now. Let's just enjoy the moment." They cuddled up together, Frank laying his hand on top of his wife's belly.

"You're going to be a father," she said, turning to kiss him.

"You've made me so happy, Autum. I promise that I'll always be there for you both." He lowered his head to kiss her belly.

Autum started to laugh but she knew why Frank had said what he had just said. Even though she had not known she was pregnant before, she had still had to deal with the loss all by herself. Frank had only just got out of his coma. Even then, she remembered how he was when he found out.

"It's going to be fine, Frank, I know it." They continued to embrace for a while longer.

"Can we keep this to ourselves? You know, just until we get the first scan out of the way. I just want to make sure everything is OK," Frank explained.

Frank knew that perhaps his words had come out wrong but he was worried about what had happened before. He couldn't let anything like that happen again. Not this time. He would be even more vigilant about Isobelle, about everything, than before. He would not lose his unborn child. He ran his hand through his hair, thinking about what he was going to do next. He knew Isobelle would be away for a two days, but when she came back Frank was due to leave to go to Barcelona two weeks later. *Let's hope Autum keeps her promise and tells no one.*

Frank was too excited and worried to sleep so he left Autum in bed. She really did look drained after her ordeal. He retired to his study to work and take his mind off things but he struggled to concentrate. He checked his watch and thought about ringing his parents. He knew it wouldn't hurt, as they were so far away and Autum would never find out, he hoped. He dialled their number.

"Hi, Mum," he said in a joyous mood.

"How are you, son?"

"Not bad at all. Where's Dad?" he asked.

"I'll go and get him. Is everything fine, son?" He could hear in her voice that she sounded worried.

"Couldn't be better." He found himself laughing.

"Son?" was all he heard down the phone.

"Dad, put yourself on loud speaker. I want Mum to hear this."

"We can hear you son," his mum replied.

"You're going to be grandparents." He heard his mother screeching down the phone.

"Congratulations, son," was all his father could say, his wife still shouting joyously in the background.

"You can't let Autum know I told you, as we've said we're waiting to tell people after she goes for her first scan in a few weeks." Frank sounded like a naughty school-boy.

"You're secret's safe with us," said his dad, chuckling.

Frank spent some time talking to his parents, letting them know about everything that had happened recently. He spoke about what had happened with Isobelle and felt the weight being lifted from his shoulders. He ended the call. He did not see Autum until he turned his chair back around.

"Jesus! You nearly scared the shit out of me!" he said, rising from his seat.

"'Keep it a secret,' you said. 'Don't tell anyone,' you said." She put her hands on her hips.

"I'm sorry. I didn't think you would mind if I told my parents. After all, they are so far away – no one will know." He knew it was a lame excuse but he thought he would give it a try.

"So I can tell *my* parents?" she asked, shaking her head in disbelief.

"Of course you can," he said, feeling as though he had been given a get-out-of-jail-free card.

Autum sat on Frank's lap as she told her parents the good news. He felt bad she had not been with him to tell his. After that, they both went back to bed and started to prepare for work the next day.

As Autum left for work, she found that her very big security guard was back in play. He was waiting outside for her next to the car. No train then, she thought to herself, as she said her greetings and got in the car. This explained why Frank had left before her: to avoid her wrath. He's so dead, she thought as the car drove off, pulling out her phone.

Frank had a lot to do over the next few weeks and found that the day seemed to be going by quickly. Frank had made sure that Isobelle's access restrictions had been put in place. He had a catch-up meeting with Mrs Lorenzo and made sure that she would keep him informed. Isobelle and the others had arrived safely in Wales. Frank's phone went off throughout the morning and he didn't need to look at it to know it was his wife. She was going to kill him, for sure, but he was going to make sure that if he was going down, it would be after he had ridden that sexy body over and over again, on the floor, the bed, in the study and in the bathroom, until he was drained of energy. Frank felt his trousers tighten, forgetting where he was. Luckily, he was in his own office, hidden behind his desk. He stood up to adjust himself and checked his phone. *Eight missed calls.* He laughed. He was so dead.

Autum arrived home just before seven. Rosetta greeted her and told her that Frank was going to be

194

working late. She laughed and Rosetta gave her a "what's-so-funny?" look. She quickly got her keys and turned straight back out of the door. Mr Big-and-protective bodyguard was still sitting in the car in the driveway, talking on the phone. As she got into the car, he stopped the conversation.

"Where are we off to?" he asked. She smiled as they headed towards Frank's office.

Frank was unaware that his wife was in the building, let alone heading towards his office. He thought that by the time he got home, she would be too tired to argue and would just accept that he was making sure she would be protected at all times. As he rubbed at his forehead, he heard a knock at his door. He thought it might be security, doing a floor check to see who was still left in the building. Then he recognised those sexy legs.

Shit, he thought, his eyes scanning up her body until they met her glare.

"Hiding at work now, are we?" She approached his desk.

"I… I have a lot to do before I leave." Frank couldn't believe she was making him stutter.

"I don't need protecting like that. You are making it obvious. He's not exactly discreet!" That made Frank laugh.

"He's not going away, honey. Not for a long time." He walked round the desk and met her.

It's nice to see her here, he thought. Since she had been running the Birmingham office, he had forgotten what it was like to see her at work. He went in for a kiss but she turned to the side and he just about caught her cheek.

"Not going to get round me like that," she said.

Frank loved a challenge and he knew that she had just set him one without even realising it.

Frank collected his belongings with a smile and phoned the bodyguard to let him off duty for the night. As he guided his wife out of the building, he was humming to himself.

"What are you so happy about?" Autum asked.

"I have every reason to be happy: a lovely wife… No, a pregnant lovely wife!" They headed home.

Autum noticed how smug Frank had been since they left the office. She knew her husband well and knew he always thought he was in control. She was about to change that. They grabbed a bite to eat, relaxed for a few hours, then retired to bed around ten-thirty. Autum pulled on a show-stopper of an outfit and watched Frank's reaction when he came out of the shower.

Frank had wanted to pat himself on the back when he realised that Autum would have to cave into his request. It was only that her safety was his number one priority; he couldn't understand why she never thought of it that way. With a towel wrapped around his waist, he entered the bedroom. When he looked up, he saw his wife wearing her gold bustier, his favourite, and some skimpy knickers. I am so in control, he thought to himself as he approached her.

"You know I love this outfit," he said, his hot breath hitting her.

"How much do you love it?" she whispered back, nibbling his ear.

"I love it more on the floor," he said, starting to unzip it.

Autum was smiling to herself as she allowed Frank to let the bustier slip to the floor.

"Get rid of the bodyguard." She released his towel.

Frank realised that Autum was playing dirty but he never lost. *Ever.*

"We can talk about it later," he said, as he slipped his hands around her panties and started to pull them down. He watched her step out of them.

"If that's what you want." She slowly wrapped her hand around his hard cock and gave it a squeeze.

Frank let out a breath and felt his cock harden more. He watched Autum release it and turn to head towards the bed. He was laughing so much inside that he was struggling to contain it.

As Autum headed towards the bed, she was grinning from ear to ear. *Does he really think it was going to be that easy?* She put her hand under her pillow, pulled out a negligée, slipped it quickly over her head and stepped into bed.

"Good night, darling." She felt her voice going higher as she held herself back from laughing.

Frank stopped in his track just inches from the bed. *Have I just been played?* His cock was throbbing for contact. It was pleading with him to make things right. It wanted action and he nearly bent down his head to explain. *Am I on the verge of talking to my cock? What the hell has she done to me?* He started to lose focus. Autum was curled up under the sheets, laughing at him, he was sure. She was getting better at reading him. Impossible, he thought. His cock wanted action and he wanted action, so he would listen to what she had to say. He would not agree to anything but he would listen. He slipped into bed and wrapped his arm

197

around her waist. He went via her breasts and stroked her nipples. They were hard. So weak… he thought to himself as he felt her shifting.

"I'm trying to protect the both of you," he said, his hand stroking up and down her side.

"I know you are but I'm not ready for it yet." She was still facing away from him.

"What do you want me to do?" His hand slipped under her and began to stroke her ass.

"Just give me a few months," she said, struggling to concentrate with his roaming hand.

"I will give you a month, at most." He pressed his body more into her, his cock hard in her back.

"More," she shot back quickly.

"Oh, I'm going to give you more." He spun her round and dived on top of her.

Autum thought she had got him for once but found he had just pipped her to the post. She couldn't recover with his body pressed on top of her, the way his fingers were in between her legs. She knew she was doomed and just let nature take its course as he slipped her negligée above her waist.

Frank felt like an "Alpha" as he worked his wife's body. He promised he would be more guarded if she pulled a stunt like that again. *If she had held out, she might have won.* He continued his onslaught between her legs. He so loved this woman. He guided his hungry cock inside her, taking his time to make love to her, observing how her eyes rolled back, the way her head tilted to the side so that he could nuzzle her neck, the moans she made for him, the way she dug her nails into his back, making him even harder and the way she grabbed his ass, pushing him deeper into her. He took her mouth hard, plunging his tongue inside her. He could feel her heart beating rapidly. She was ready, she was coming, she was his. As she erupted around him, he felt his own release and followed. Frank rolled off her and she turned to face him, the rising and falling of their chests showing they had not yet come down from their high.

"You know you nearly had me?" Frank said with a smile.

"Next time, I won't be so forgiving." She slapped him playfully on the shoulder.

"So there will be a next time, eh?" He pulled her close.

Autum could only shake her head in disbelief as they continued their embrace and at last fell asleep.

Chapter Twenty

Isobelle had enjoyed her few days in Wales. She and the team had worked hard but she wanted to work even harder. Her job depended on it. Mrs Lorenzo contacted her nearly every day for an update, which she was happy to supply.

It was her first day back at work and Bob was on duty in reception. He gave her a partial smile as he issued her with her pass.

"Welcome back, Isobelle," he said, handing it to her.

"Thank you, Bob," she replied, a smile lighting up her whole face. Bob was quite happy to wipe it off.

"Your access has been restricted."

"What?" Isobelle's voice was louder than she had wanted it to be, as people were walking past her in reception.

Bob ignored her.

"You only have access to the second and first floors." He smiled back at her.

Isobelle's face was on fire. *How could she? I kept my end of the bargain.* She grabbed her pass and stormed off. As she reached her floor, she knocked hard on Mrs Lorenzo's door.

"Come in." Isobelle was already through the door.

"Restricted access? When were you going to tell me?" she asked. Her voice was raised but not to the point of being disrespectful.

"Take a seat, Isobelle," said Mrs Lorenzo, standing to face her.

"I did a good job, didn't I?"

"Yes, you did but it still doesn't change the fact of what you did to Mr Howard. I fought hard to even get you to keep your job. A few restrictions are the least of your worries. Don't make me regret my decision." She stared hard at Isobelle.

Isobelle wanted to say more, wanted to challenge her, but how could she? She had got her job back and that should have been enough. But it wasn't.

"Thank you for what you did. It was just a shock, that's all," she managed to reply.

"A shock I'm sure you can adapt to. Was there anything else?" Mrs Lorenzo finally said.

"No." And with that, Isobelle got up and went back to her desk, grinding her teeth and clenching her fist.

She worked hard all morning, finding that it helped relieve some of the stress she was under. She went to lunch around one-thirty. She loved the food at her favourite café. She had steak with caramelised onions on ciabatta bread and then ordered a Strawberry and Cream Frappuccino to go. She felt a pang in her gut and felt like she was being watched. *How odd.* For a split second, she felt shocked. She was unsure where the feeling had come from. Nothing seemed out of the ordinary when she looked around, so she continued back to work, taking sips of her drink as she went. At the end of the day, Mrs Lorenzo called her in for a follow-up meeting.

"How are you feeling now?" she asked

Isobelle actually didn't know how to answer. After the initial shock and having taken out some stress on her keyboard, she felt like nothing had changed.

"Good, thanks." And that was her honest reply.

They talked for a few more minutes and then Isobelle left the office, collected her things and headed home. There she turned on the television, got herself a bottle of rosé and relaxed for the evening.

The next few weeks went by quickly and Isobelle quickly realised that she didn't even need access to the other floors. She had only used to visit them to see Autum. She stopped what she was doing and realised that she had not thought about Autum in a long time. *How strange. Maybe I should thank Frank for giving me that kick up the ass to realise what I had to lose.* Isobelle went for lunch with her friend Lucy, who talked for England but at least provided her with a lunch-buddy.

"So what are you up to on Friday?" Lucy asked as they sat on a bench in the grounds of the office.

"I don't know to be honest, just the usual I think: stay at home, watch a movie and drink some wine" Even as she said it, she realised she sounded like a saddo.

"Oh, that sounds interesting," said Lucy, rolling her eyes.

"Did you have something planned?"

"Not really but I wouldn't mind checking out some of the bars in the West End. What do you think?" Lucy waited eagerly for her response.

Isobelle looked over at her new friend. Is she a loner like me? she thought to herself. Either way, she had nothing better to do and it might be fun.

"Why not!" she said, smiling.

Autum couldn't believe how quickly time had flown by. She was lucky that Frank had given her a bit of space with the bodyguard but now that she had reached thirteen weeks, would that change? They headed into the hospital and asked to see Dr Keen. Autum was also due for her scan. They waited to be seen and filled in some additional paperwork.

"Mrs Autum Howard?" she heard a nurse say.

"Yes, that's me." She stood up and followed the nurse to a private room.

Frank held her hand. He wasn't sure who was more nervous: he or Autum. He watched the nurse talk to his anxious wife as she lay down. He watched her lift up her top and pull her trousers slightly down below her waist. The nurse placed tissue on her. Autum found herself jumping when the gel was squirted on to her. She mentioned how cold it was as the nurse rubbed it across her belly. Frank held his wife's hand as they heard the loud, quick heartbeats of their child. Then the nurse turned the screen to face them and they saw the first image of their unborn child.

"Oh God, look…" Autum turned to Frank.

Frank stood there watching the screen, looking at his child. He was so proud that he couldn't speak, only stare. He turned to his wife and kissed the top of her head.

"Our son…" he said, eventually. "Or daughter!" The nurse and Autum smiled.

Once Autum had cleaned herself up, they waited for the pictures and then went to see Dr Keen. They didn't stay too long with him as he only wanted to check to see if Autum had had any more spells and give her a quick once over. Nothing is better than this moment, thought Frank, staring at the photograph of the scan and arguing with Autum about whether it looked like a boy or a girl.

Autum had kept her promise and not said a word to anyone other than her parents. But now she had passed twelve weeks and the baby was fine, Frank agreed that she could tell Rebecca. Frank was due to leave for Barcelona in two days' time, so Autum needed to make sure to ask Rebecca if she could stay over until he got back. The last thing she wanted was to have the hulk watching over her. When they got home, the first thing Frank did was call out Rosetta's name as he rushed into the kitchen. *It sounds like he's the one having the baby!*

"Look, Rosetta…" He held the picture of the scan out to her, Autum standing by his side.

Rosetta looked at the picture and started to babble on in Spanish. Then, before Frank could respond, she held his face with both her hands and gave him a kiss on both cheeks. Then she nudged him out of the way to do the same for Autum. Then she really started to get going, demanding that Frank stop working late in "that room", as she called it, and insisting that Autum put her feet up. On and on she went, even changing her entire plan for what they would have for dinner.

"Have you ever seen anyone that happy?" said Frank. Autum turned to face him.

"Yes, I have."

Autum had a quick shower then relaxed on the bed. She pulled out her phone and dialled Rebecca's number.

"Hi, Rebecca."

"Hi, Autum, have you recovered from the dinner?" She started to laugh.

"Oh God, I had forgotten about that." She thought back to how much she had drunk.

Rebecca laughed again.

"What's up?"

"I wanted you to be the first to know, after my parents of course, that I am pregnant."

Autum didn't hear Rebecca respond at first.

"Rebecca? Are you still there?"

"I'm so happy for you, I really am." Rebecca's voice started to shake.

"Don't! You're gonna set me off…" They both started to laugh.

They talked for a while longer and Autum asked about staying over for a few days. She informed Rebecca about the bodyguard. She had managed to ditch him so far but she was not sure how much longer that would last. Frank entered the bedroom, saw his wife giggling on the phone and left her to it.

Frank took a picture of the scan photograph and sent it to his parents. It took them about thirty minutes to call back and then it was Frank's turn to laugh down the phone. They were already trying to say who it looked like and Frank could only shake his head and laugh some more.

Frank had started to prepare himself for his trip. Everything was in hand and even though he had not rehired the bodyguard for Autum, he felt confident that she would be alright going to work and staying at Rebecca's house. He had asked Julian to keep an eye on them both as well.

Autum had come home at her usual time and heard laughter in the kitchen. She wasn't sure if they had a guest over – she could not think who it could be. To her surprise, it was José. Rosetta was taking some time out to visit her family and Frank was organising for her to leave as soon as she could.

As they exchanged greetings, José said his congratulations. All Autum could think of was all the lovely meals that he would be preparing for them soon. They spent an hour or so chatting before he left, Autum wasn't that hungry and wanted just to have a light snack. She told Rosetta not to worry, as she was happy to just put something together from the fridge. She was shocked that all her treats were still in the fridge, not like last time. She made herself a ham, cheese and pickle sandwich and a hot chocolate with cream and marshmallows. Rosetta just shook her head in disbelief, making her smile. The evening went by quickly and the night even more quickly, as Frank left his mark on her body before he slipped away to the airport.

"I'll ring you when I arrive," he whispered before he slipped towards the door.

"Where's my goodbye kiss?" said Autum groggily.

"Still all over your body," Frank replied as he blew her a kiss and left the bedroom.

207

Yes, his kisses really were all over her body and she was still aching.

"Love you," she said, slightly raising her head, as he shut the door behind him and she drifted back off to sleep.

Autum slept heavily and woke up feeling drained. She quickly had a shower and prepared herself for her daily routine. The house was quiet but at least she had Rosetta to keep her company for breakfast, which consisted of two poached eggs, crispy bacon, grilled tomatoes and a selection of wild mushrooms with two rounds of toast and juice.

There was no sign of her usual latte. She sighed as she could really have done with a caffeine rush; she wasn't going to argue with Rosetta though! She was sure that between her and José, a few more of her things would disappear over time. They were probably trying to break her in slowly.

She knew that the rest of the girls had been told of her news and that they would be passing by on Friday night. It was just after lunchtime when Frank rung to say that he had arrived safely. They chatted but not for long and she told him that her morning latte had mysteriously disappeared.

"You know it's not good for you. Or our son," he replied.

"Or daughter!" she corrected him. He chuckled and had to then quickly end the call as he was going into a meeting.

"I'll call you later," he said and hung up.

Autum got back into the swing of things and went from meeting to meeting and her day was soon over. For once, she actually missed the bodyguard, as she would have loved a lift back in a car, where she could take off her shoes and fall asleep.

When she got home, she quickly grabbed some clothes for the next few days, then headed straight to Rebecca's house.

On Friday, Autum only worked until two before catching the train to Rebecca's. She was so looking forward to seeing the girls and chatting about her pregnancy while eating all of the things that would soon be banned from her mouth.

Isobelle and Lucy were preparing for their night out. Isobelle was showing Lucy some of her outfits, trying to decide if they were trendy enough. For each one, Lucy gave her a nod or a shake of her head. Before long, her bed was just a pile of clothes but she knew exactly what her outfit would be. As she glammed herself up, she felt happy with how she looked. It had been a long time since she had seen herself like this and she looked good. She topped up her lipstick before heading outside for a cab. Friday nights in the West End were really busy and she loved the noise of the city.

As Lucy and Isobelle drank and partied, they were approached by two good-looking guys.

"Can we buy you a drink, ladies," said the first, a hottie with a tight top and bulging muscles.

Lucy was quite drunk and was throwing her arms over his mate's neck. It was in that split second that it dawned on her what Autum must have seen all those years ago. Isobelle saw how the guy was looking at Lucy, in the same way that Jack had looked at her three years earlier – disgusted. It felt like déjà vu. She made her excuses, dragged Lucy away from them and headed for the bar. She asked the waiter for shots and they knocked them back, then another. Isobelle wanted to erase all those bad memories.

"Slow down, Isobelle, we have all night," said Lucy.

But Isobelle was now past caring. As the night went on, she drank more and more until she slipped and twisted her ankle.

"Come on, let's get you home," said Lucy, hanging on to her friend and flagging down a black cab.

They talked about the night they had just had and the hunky guys they had met and before they knew it they had arrived outside Isobelle's apartment. Lucy helped to get her upstairs and into her bedroom.

"I'll bring you a bucket, just in case," she said, laughing.

"You're such a good mate," Isobelle replied, incoherently.

"You sure you'll be OK? I can stay if you want."

"I'll be fine. Just make sure you shut the door properly before you leave. Thanks again for tonight." And she curled up in bed, fully clothed except for her shoes.

"Oh I forgot to tell you the latest gossip. You know Rebecca's friend, not sure of her name, who works in the Birmingham office…"

"What about her?" Isobelle raised herself up on her elbows, now fully alert. She knew Lucy was talking about Autum.

"What is her name? For the life of me, it's at the tip of my tongue."

"What about her?" Isobelle said again, jumping up painfully from bed and shaking Lucy.

"OK, calm down! What the hell is up with you?" said Lucy and shrugged out of her hold.

"Sorry. Just wanted you to tell me what you heard, that's all. You're keeping me in suspense here!"

Lucy looked excited.

"Well, it's all around the office that she is pregnant!"

Isobelle felt the bile rising in her stomach. She held out one hand to steady herself on the wall. Lucy was right there beside her and managed to help her to the bathroom before she threw up. She was sick for some time before she motioned Lucy to help her up.

"You don't look too well," said Lucy.

Isobelle splashed her face with some water and rinsed out her mouth before heading back to the bedroom.

"I'm fine, just too much drink." Isobelle knew that was half-true. But it was the fact that Autum was pregnant and she wasn't that had made her stomach churn even more.

As Lucy continued to talk, Isobelle started feeling light-headed. She felt her heart speed up but blamed her shock and having been sick. But as she tried to make her way into bed, she passed out. The next thing she saw was Lucy beside her bed. But she wasn't in her own bed, she was in hospital.

"What the hell happened?"

She smelled of sick and it was making her want to vomit all over again.

"You threw up, then fainted and when you fainted, you banged your head on the side of your table. God, the noise was so loud and when you wouldn't

211

wake up, I called an ambulance. You scared the shit out of me!" Lucy spoke without taking in a breath.

"Thanks," was all Isobelle could muster. Her mouth tasted foul and her voice sounded rough.

When the doctor came in, Isobelle could see the disgust on his face. Another Friday-night drunk, he was probably thinking to himself. And he was right.

"Miss Isobelle Jackson, you gave yourself a nasty bump on the head," he said, as he came over to inspect her. He got out a flashlight out and flicked it on in each of her eyes. "What's the last thing you remember?"

Isobelle felt like a school-kid, the way he said her name out in full. She went through what she remembered and thought she did pretty well but she couldn't recall the last few hours.

"There is some swelling at the side of your head, so, to be on the safe side, we will run you up for some tests and if everything is OK, we will let you go home. Just make sure that if you feel any dizziness in the next twenty-four hours, you get it checked out. I will get someone to come for you in a short while." But he never got a chance to leave because the next thing he heard was Lucy screaming. Isobelle's eyes had rolled back and her head was hanging off the side of the bed.

Chapter Twenty-One

Frank's trip to Barcelona went off without any hitches. He rung Autum quite a few times whilst he was there. He had started to relax more, as she seemed to be coping fine. Every night before he went to bed, he took out and stared at the photograph of his "son". And even as he thought the word, he could hear Autum correcting him and he smiled to himself. He was heading home in the morning and was glad that nothing had happened whilst he was away. The next day, he went back to the little shop he had found on his last visit, hidden away, and smiled at the shop-assistant in recognition. He took his time, exploring and picking up items, and then headed to the airport.

Autum enjoyed seeing all of her friends again. Dionne, Imogen and Emily had all bought little gifts out of sheer excitement.

"Show us the picture then," said Emily, as they all looked on.

Autum searched her bag but couldn't find it. She started to panic, thinking she might have lost it. When she rang Frank to tell him, he confessed to taking it, saying he hadn't thought she would mind. She was just happy it was safe.

The girls then asked when the baby was due and she told them it would be around the 10th September. They insisted on seeing her belly, which, to be honest, only had a very small bump. To the girls, however, it was still a big thing. They laughed and ate and talked about everything and as they drank, Autum held up her glass of sparkling juice and they all said, "Cheers!" to "junior". Before long, she was saying her goodbyes and packing to go back home. After the girls left, Rebecca had a talk with Autum.

"Everybody's talking about your pregnancy in the office; it's like the biggest news ever," she said, her voice rising an octave.

Autum could only think of one person that might not take the news so well, Isobelle.

"I know what you're thinking…" said Rebecca.

"You don't think she would harm me or my child do you?" And that was a question that neither one of them could answer, no matter how much Rebecca tried to reassure her best friend.

Isobelle had been off sick since her night out with Lucy two weeks earlier. She had received shocking news that night and was struggling to come to terms with it. Lucy had sent her some flowers and wished her a speedy recovery and she was due back in the office on Monday so would catch up with her then. She had found out that Autum was just over four months pregnant and was looking *swell*, according to her sources at work. Her breathing quickened as she pictured the happy family. She got dressed and decided to get out of the apartment as it was suffocating her. She went to visit Jack's grave but could not get any peace there either so left soon afterwards. Everywhere she looked around her, she saw pregnant mothers, mothers pushing prams and mothers with children.

"Today," she said aloud, "is the beginning of a new life. I just need to close down this chapter, which has been going on for far too long." Isobelle went back to work as normal and spent the next few days working late, catching up on work she had missed. She blamed herself for having had so much time off so pushed herself to complete her outstanding projects with short deadlines and pushy project leaders. She wasn't eating or sleeping well, some days only having four hours or so. She never had much time to see Lucy outside of work and even her boss noticed the change in her. Mrs Lorenzo didn't say much though as no matter what was going on, Isobelle never missed a deadline. She finally found time to take a lunch break and headed to her favourite place to eat. As she started to devour her pulled-pork bap, she recognised Rebecca's voice and turned around, seeing her walk towards the counter, laughing down the phone as she scanned the menu.

"What do you mean you have a craving for pickled onions? That's so disgusting!" Rebecca laughed.

They caught each other's eyes.

"Yes, I'm in your favourite café ordering lunch. It's not the same without you. Some people should not be allowed to eat in here." She glanced back at Isobelle, who had not stopped staring.

Isobelle continued to force down her food, finding it hard to swallow. She listened to Rebecca taunting her to her friend down the phone, making her feel worthless. *I'll show you, you worthless bitch.* She picked up her drink, discarded the bap she was enjoying and walked out of the café.

Rebecca had ordered her lunch to go and was snacking on it on the way back to work. As she waited to cross the road, she felt a hot breath against her ear.

"You're next," was all Isobelle said before she disappeared into the crowd.

Rebecca knew when she heard the voice that it was Isobelle. She felt her whole body shudder with fear. She had not felt this scared since the incident with Jack and he had messed her up big-time. The light turned green and the crowd pushed her forward. On the other side, she immediately rang Frank and then headed straight for his office.

Frank was pacing his office and when Rebecca had arrived, he was not far from pouncing on her.

"What did you do to provoke her?" Frank wanted to say more but this was not the time.

"Nothing! I swear. I was speaking to Autum before I got into the café and continued a while longer inside. I noticed Isobelle giving me daggers so I did the same and continued ordering. I may have commented that certain people should not be allowed to eat there but no way could she have heard that or realised it was aimed at her!" Rebecca was beginning to realise she had just triggered a time bomb.

"Do you know what you have done, Rebecca? You have woken up a dormant volcano." He slumped into his chair and wondered how this was going to affect him and Autum. "You better get Julian to take you home tonight and just remain vigilant, OK?"

Rebecca went back to work but felt on edge for the rest of the afternoon. Any noise she heard made her jump. She was happy when Julian came into view and they both left together. But once she got home, she still didn't feel safe and even though she had Julian for company, sleeping was not much better either.

By the time Frank got home, he felt like he had the weight of the world on his shoulders. *Should I mention this to her?* He knew he had no choice. If he didn't and she found out through Rebecca his life would not be worth living. As she approached him in his study, he saw how her body was now changing shape: a little bump visible, her face even more beautiful and her boobs even bigger. Frank nearly forgot the reason why he needed to speak to her as his eyes focused on those boobs bouncing towards him. *Focus.*

"I know that look," said Autum, raising her eyebrows.

"What look?" said Frank. He wasn't sure if she meant that she knew he wanted to fuck her like mad or that she knew he was hiding something from him.

"That look when you want to devour my body and leave me unable to walk." She folded her arms across her chest.

Frank wished it was that simple. His cock went into overdrive when she crossed her arms across her chest. It made her boobs almost spill out of her top. But then he thought about Isobelle again and all thoughts of his wife laying on his desk with her mouth around his cock vanished.

"We need to talk." Yep, that doused the fire big-time.

"Oh, is everything alright?" She walked around his desk and sat on his lap.

"It's Isobelle, I think she may be after Rebecca." Autum shot up from his lap.

"Sit back down," he said and told her everything that he knew about the incident.

Autum was quiet for a moment before she spoke.

"She didn't mention this to me and I only spoke to her a few hours ago. What does this all mean for us?"

Frank couldn't answer her because he didn't know the answer himself.

"Maybe this will all blow over. We all know that she must know you're pregnant and I've not had any concerns up until now. From what I can gather, she was involved in some sort of accident and was off work for a while but returned today. Julian is looking after Rebecca and that is all I know so far."

Autum thought about what had been said and realised that Frank had been right so far. She was four months gone and Isobelle had not posed a threat to her up to this point. Maybe this was her turning point. Now that she knew Autum was pregnant, maybe she would leave her and Frank alone. *Just as long as Rebecca doesn't pay the price instead...* Autum stayed with Frank and they talked about doing up the nursery, baby names, everything baby-related. Frank was feeling happy when Autum finally burned herself out and went to bed. He had been worried that she was saying one thing and thinking another but he knew that was not the case this time around: he could see it on her face. He thought about hiring security again but like Autum said, they had not seen Isobelle do anything. Yes, in light of this recent event, he needed to keep his guard up but until Autum felt like she was not safe, he would reluctantly keep his promise. And with that thought, he left his study and joined his wife in bed.

Isobelle was mad that Rebecca had got to her the way she did. *How dare she!* She continued putting on a brave face in the office. This was better than anything she could have hoped for. With luck, Frank would be so busy watching Rebecca's back that he would forget to watch Autum's. All she had to do was bide her time and then strike. The rest of her afternoon went well, her mind filled with what she would like to do to them all. Frank still needed to pay for humiliating her by throwing her out of his office and banning her from certain floors. He was treating her like a convict so she might as well live up to it. She checked no one was watching and dialled the Birmingham office. She pretended to be a client and arranged for a direct meeting with Mrs Howard in New York to discuss a lucrative business opportunity. She was put on hold for some time and was worrying that she had been busted when the PA came back and slotted her in for an appointment next week. All Isobelle could do was smile. She then confirmed with the PA a hotel reservation for Autum for two nights. It had to be believable and a trip that only required one night could be dismissed or handled via a teleconference. She gave her name as Miss Angelica Thomas, representing Thomas Enterprises. She knew that they had approached Frank around a year and a half before. He had sent Autum and a small team to New York to meet with them but nothing had come of it. She knew Autum would not think anything was out of the ordinary. Isobelle was happy with her plan. She knew everything about her best friend Autum, because Autum and Isobelle had shared everything over the last three years. *Even men.* Isobelle let out a small laugh, continued making phone calls and booked herself into a different New York hotel. She just hoped Frank would allow his wife to fly.

When Autum arrived in Birmingham, she was happy to be greeted by her favourite latté. Her PA came in soon afterwards and went through her schedule over the next few days. She also mentioned a new meeting that she had booked in for Thomas Enterprises in New York. She had already made reservations at a hotel. Autum, engrossed in her latté, took a while before she processed the information. She remembered having a meeting with them years ago but was shocked that they would arrange another. She was so excited at the prospect that she phoned Frank and told him the good news.

"I'm coming with you," he informed his wife.

"Oh Frank, really? You know I can do this right?" she fired back.

"Of course you can, honey. I just think it would be nice if I came with you and we mixed business with pleasure. Tell me the date and I will make arrangements." That ended that discussion.

Once off the phone, Autum got her PA to make the additional arrangements for the trip in a week's time and no more was said.

Chapter Twenty-Two

Isobelle had booked some time off work and had organised a driver to pick Autum up from the airport and take her to her hotel. She left instructions for the driver to report back once Autum had arrived. She knew she was taking the biggest risk of all time and that there would be no going back but it didn't faze her. Everything was in place.

She had arrived in New York a day early to have some "me time". She liked being out and about and felt sexy when men walked by and gave her that lingering look. She liked how when she asked for directions, people latched on to her accent and were more than happy to help. She liked the fact that no one knew her there and that the fast pace of life was not so different from London. I could get used to living here, she thought.

Frank was busy trying to rush Autum into packing *light* for the trip. It was only going to be for two days but Autum was packing for what looked like two weeks.

"Do you really need all those shoes?" Frank was baffled.

"I've only packed four pairs, one for each day and one for each evening." She gave Frank a look that said, "You have not even seen how many outfits I've packed yet!" and smiled to herself.

Frank took out his weekend bag and placed it on the bed. He then took out two shirts and two suits, only one of which he would be wearing, and accessories to match.

"Is that all your packing?" Autum said, surprised.

"You know I pack light. I only take what is required, nothing more." He raised his eyebrows at the pile of clothes stacking up on the bed.

"Point taken," she said, laughing lightly.

They passed the night making love and woke up early to leave for the airport. It was going to be a nice break for both of them and Frank couldn't wait. They arrived and were greeted by a chauffeur with a plaque who escorted them to a waiting car. The weather was quite cold for April but they had wrapped up accordingly.

At check-in, Autum said her name and was handed a letter that confirmed she would be picked up at nine-thirty the next morning. She was glad as that gave them a day to themselves. She thought nothing more of the note and she and Frank were then shown to their suite. Frank had asked for an upgrade as he wanted to pamper his expecting wife. No expense was spared and he could not wait to brag about his up-coming fatherhood in the meeting. When the luggage was brought to their room, they quickly unpacked and ventured out. By the time they had come back to the hotel, they had just enough time to shower and change into something formal for dinner.

"They really must be serious about investing this time, don't you think?" said Autum, as she glanced around the hotel dining area, which seemed as lavish as that of the Ritz.

"I think you may be right," said Frank, taking charge of ordering appetizers and, for himself, wine.

"I can have a glass, you know. It won't do any harm," said Autum, as Frank enjoyed his drink.

"A spritzer then?" as Frank gave her that "keep-trying-love-it's-not-going-to-happen" look.

They talk about their strategic plan for the next day. They had already prepared a presentation and a Q&A session. They could not foresee anything that would catch them off guard. They had been well-prepared and were confident they would be securing a deal with Thomas Enterprises. They raised their glasses and continued to enjoy their meal.

Nine-thirty on the dot and the limo was waiting outside the hotel. The chauffeur opened the door on seeing them approach and then they pulled away. Both Frank and Autum were sharing a private joke, not taking their surrounds in. Autum cuddled up to Frank as the limo continued driving for another forty minutes.

"They must have moved offices since the last time I was here, I don't remember the drive being so long," said Autum, sitting up straight.

"I'm sure the driver knows where he's going, dear. Relax." He pulled her tighter towards him.

"Are we nearly there?" she asked, pressing the intercom to speak to the driver.

"Yes, madam," he replied.

Frank dismissed Autum's concerns as nerves. They had asked for her especially and she was probably feeling the pressure.

"You're gonna nail this, love. This one is all yours." He kissed her on the forehead.

"I hope so, I'm just so nervous. I didn't get it last time. Maybe..." Frank cut her off.

"This one's in the bag." He tilted her head towards him and kissed her on the lips. The kiss deepened, his heart started to race and he heard a low moan escape her. They remembered where they were and broke away.

"Frank, this is so not the place! And look at my lipstick!" She dug it out of her purse to top up and caught her breath.

"You look like you needed to relax," said Frank, wiping the red stain off his lips with his thumb. Before they could say another word, the limo slowed down and stopped. They heard the driver's door shut and then their door opened. Frank looked at his wife.

"Good luck," he said, and they both exited the limo. They looked around to see a newly constructed building before them and another limo a few feet away. They walked towards the other limo as their own drove away behind them.

"Do you think these are their new offices?" Autum asked but Frank did not answer. Instead, he reached for his wife's hand and continued to walk. A chauffeur exited the vehicle and opened the passenger door. They both stopped. A pair of four inch heels with beautiful red soles, attached to the longest pair of legs

Autum had ever seen, stepped out. This must be Angelica, thought Autum, noting how slim and sexy this woman was. She had long, flowing, brunette, curly locks and large, dark sunglasses. The limo drove away. Autum and Frank shook hands with her.

"Angelica, I presume." Isobelle smiled at him, before putting on her best New York accent and ushering them towards the building, even giving them both hard hats.

Isobelle explained the site's construction and the company's ambitious plans for their new headquarters, what they didn't know was that the building had been shut down as the construction company had gone bust and the building not classified as being safe as she directed them into the building. Frank and Autum were utterly drawn in by the size of the building and the floor plan. They moved away some plastic sheets, heading towards the lifts. Once inside, Isobelle pressed the button for the seventeenth floor.

"This will look great when it's finished," said Autum.

"Will the meeting be taking place here?" asked Frank, going into business-mode.

"No, I was just asked to show you around our new offices so that you could see the business-potential of what you would be investing in." Isobelle had really done her homework and was shocked that she had not given the game away.

Frank was getting a little bored now. A building was a building and he got what this brunette bimbo was trying to say.

"Can we head back now? My wife is expecting and I don't want her to breathe in all of this dust."

"Frank," said Autum, nudging him.

Isobelle turned around and looked at Autum. It was the first proper look she had given her for such a long time. She noticed how good Autum was looking, even though she still could not see that she was pregnant through her figure-hugging coat.

"You look so well. How far gone are you?" It was nearly killing her to say each word.

"Just over four months." Autum put her hand to her belly and smiled.

Isobelle walked over to her and gave her a hug. "It looks like it's going to be a double celebration, isn't that right, Frank?" Isobelle said the last few words in her normal accent.

Autum turned around to look at the woman standing next to her as she took off her sunglasses. Isobelle's grip around her waist was getting tighter; she tried to move out of her hold.

"Oh not so fast, Autum. Aren't you going to say congratulations to your best friend?"

"Isobelle! It can't be!" Shocked, Autum started to look more closely at her. She nearly fainted as she became certain who it was.

Frank made a move towards them.

"Now, now, Frank, you wouldn't want to hurt your baby-mothers now, would you?" She started to laugh.

"No fucking way are you pregnant, you delusional bitch!"

"Always full of love, aren't you, Frank?"

"Frank, what is she talking about?" Autum pleaded. Isobelle was now holding her by the hair.

"How the fuck do I know what goes on in that fucked-up brain of hers?" He stepped closer and she yanked Autum's hair back even more.

Isobelle took something from her pocket and showed it to Autum: a scan picture.

"She's pregnant" replied Autum, clearly shocked.

"It could be anyones, she already proved she's not loyal"

"Don't you think he looks like his daddy?" she said, throwing it towards Frank.

Frank picked it up and looked at it.

"I feel sorry for the poor child; they don't know what they're in for."

"You should know, Frank. Don't you remember when you came round my apartment?"

Autum stopped breathing for a second, racking her brains. Frank stopped breathing as well, realising what Isobelle had done…

"You fucking bitch!" he shouted, lunging at her. She ducked behind Autum.

"I see your memory has come back," said Isobelle, starting to laugh.

"You drugged me, you bitch" he said, his hands clenched into fists.

"How I remember it, you couldn't get enough of me. The taste of your cock in my mouth…"

"Don't listen to her, Autum!" Frank was on the verge of losing his temper.

"Didn't he tell you how he sucked my breasts? The way he moaned when I rode him hard over and over again?" Isobelle's mouth was right next to Autum's ear.

Frank looked over at his wife, tears streaming down her face. He had told her the truth but it was unbearable for her to hear it from her, twisted with her lies. Isobelle had now got her ultimate revenge.

"Speak to me, Autum," He fell to his knees, the pain he felt, was a form of punishment that shot up his body.

Isobelle still was not done yet.

"You know, Autum, I can understand why you loved Frank so much. His cock was so delicious when I sucked him dry and when he fucked my ass, well, that nearly took my breath away. And now I am carrying his child, I hope to get my fair share of that cock whenever I want it." Isobelle was so caught up in her warped mind that she did not see the elbow heading towards her face.

"You evil fucking bitch," said Autum as her elbow connected.

Isobelle cried out as her grip loosened enough for Autum to face her head on.

"How dare you drug my husband, then rape him and claim that child is his!" She smacked her right in the face.

"It is his. I swear it's the truth," Isobelle shouted, trying to get Autum in a choke-hold.

"The truth? Don't make me laugh. You're a whore, Isobelle, always have been, always will be – sleeping with anyone to get what you want!"

Frank was watching on bended knees the struggle between the two of them; As they fought, Isobelle thought over what Autum had said and remembered sleeping with Jason. Jason! How could she have forgotten about him? Could *he* be the father? She felt a fist hit her by the eye, which brought her back to the present.

Isobelle dragged Autum to the floor and quickly jumped on top of her. She grabbed her by the head and was about to bash it into the ground when the floor colasped below them sending them down the next level, Frank leapt up and jump down, knocking her away. He held her hands above her head, as she frantically tried to kick him off.

"Call the police, Autum!" He looked over to see his wife, curled into a ball, clutching her stomach.

"Autum!" And without a second glance, he jumped off Isobelle and headed towards her. Isobelle did not waste the opportunity and quickly got up. She looked around for anything she could find to use as a weapon, she saw scaffolding, wood and sheeting all around her and smiled.

As Frank grabbed Autum and rested her head in his lap, he did not see Isobelle approach from behind.

"Tell me where it hurts."

"I'm fine, Frank, I think it may have been just the shock of seeing that bitch."

Frank turned around quickly but could not see any sign of Isobelle. He grabbed his phone and dialled 911.

"Hello, I want to report a kidnapping..." He did not get the chance to continue.

"Frank!" was all he heard Autum scream, as he dropped his phone and felt himself being suffocated with some heavy-duty plastic sheeting.

"Why can't you just be happy for me? All I ever wanted was to become a mother, have someone to look after, to love. You took Jack from me, but here you are, happy with a pregnant wife and rubbing it in my face that I will never have this" said Isobelle, as she dragged Frank along the floor and away from Autum. Frank struggled to breathe. He tried to loosen the grip around his neck and control his breathing at the same time. He couldn't see much due to the mist forming in front of his face. All he knew was that he was moving further and further away and if he did not do something soon, this would be the last time he saw his wife.

He found himself getting weaker, his arms struggling to stay up. He could hear Autum's screams fading into the background of his mind. He knew he was drifting, knew he couldn't tell his wife how much he loved her. He hoped at least she would survive and bring up their child with both of their love. He pictured what his son would look like. Yes, he was definitely a *he*. He found himself smiling at the thought of Autum correcting him. Beautiful blond hair, hazel eyes and a cute little nose, just like his mum… That was all he pictured as he took in a breath and his world went blank.

Isobelle was sweating and panting after fighting to keep hold of Frank for that long. It was only adrenaline that had kept her strong. Gone were her shoes the pain running through her bare feet from the debris that had been left on the floor. She got her breath back, letting Frank's body slump to the floor.

"Frank!" Autum screamed, rising from the floor.

"Payback's a bitch," was all Isobelle said, letting out a hysterical laugh.

Autum took the sheeting from around Frank's face and just stared at him. He couldn't leave her, not now. Their baby wanted a father and she needed a husband. She opened his mouth trying to give him the kiss of life, she shook him to get him to try and wake up. Then she lifted Frank's head to rest under her neck. She thought she felt air but then Isobelle's voice cut through her.

"Now you know what it feels like to lose someone you love." There was a smirk on her face.

"He did not attack you or threaten to kill you or your family. What Jack did was not the same and you know it." She spoke between sobs.

"Really? That's not how I remember it." She pulled out her phone.

Autum watched Isobelle dial and was shocked to hear her next words.

"Help me, please. I've been kidnapped. They're trying to kill me and my baby!" Her voice took on a life of its own. Isobelle turned around and smiled at Autum.

"You fucking bitch!" She let go of Frank abruptly as she got up and realised his head would have hit the floor hard but dived for Isobelle, knocking the phone out of her hands as the two of them wrestled. Autum slammed her into the scaffolding but Isobelle was far from defeated. With a backhander, she hit Autum hard across the face, making her let go and giving Isobelle valuable time to grab on to her hair.

"You know I was always the better fighter," she said, as she dragged Autum across the room.
Autum tried not to focus on the pain of her hair being pulled out. She tried to balance her weight out by keeping up with being dragged.

"You won't get away with this, Isobelle," she said, wrapping her hands around Isobelle's.

"Get away with what? Murder? Well you seem to have done pretty well so far; care to give me some tips?"

Isobelle was dragging her to some open space. There was a half-built wall, then nothing. She intended to push her off the edge. *She's going to kill me.* She fought harder to gain control. She hit out many times but nothing connected and she just heard a laugh now from Isobelle. She looked at the floor but again there

231

was nothing there to help. Then, at last, she thought of something.

"Aarghh!" A high-pitched scream left Isobelle's mouth. Autum had pierced her foot with her heel. She felt Isobelle release her hair but she only just had time to right herself before Isobelle charged into her again, sending them both out on to the scaffolding. Dust, bolts, wooden planks and metal shook but yet the women continued to fight.

"Once I finish with you, I will shove Frank off as well so you can both die in each other's arms," said Isobelle.

"The only one dying today will be you. I'm sure Jack will be glad of the company. But then again, would he really want to be stuck with you in death? I mean, everyone needs a break, right!" replied Autum.

That was the last insult Isobelle was going to take, a punch to the stomach saw to that. But as they fought, shouted and screamed, neither woman saw something else that was happening. Frank had arched his back and taken in the biggest gasp of air imaginable. He had lost his bearings for a few seconds but then, as he looked around, he saw them both tangled up in each other so close to the edge. He crawled towards them, dragging himself along the floor. They were fighting like two grown men. He knew Autum was fighting for her life and for their unborn child. *Was this what she had to do with Jack?* A chill ran down his spine. This time, he would be there to help. *This time, she won't face it alone.*

Isobelle stood and towered over Autum, bruises visible on both of them. Blood and dust coated her foot but she felt no pain.

"How you ever thought you would defeat me, Autum, I will never know. Do you know how long I have waited for this moment? This is better than even I had planned it to be. And to think, you will never see my baby grow up. I want you to think about the fact that it is Frank's offspring I will be raising." She rubbed her belly. "The mistress and the jealous wife. That's how it'll be portrayed. Sounds good, don't you think?"

Autum did not respond. Why would she respond to someone so deluded and so deranged? Every extra second gave her the chance to recover. She turned her head to see how close they were to the edge of the wall.

"Do your worst, Isobelle. I don't care anymore. You see, whatever you do to me will not change the fact that Jack loved me. It won't change the fact that he was probably glad for the release from living with someone he barely even liked…"

"He loved me!" Isobelle shouted back.

"I think we both know that's not what he said before he died," Autum fired back. She was not sure why she found herself lighting the fuse on dynamite but she continued.

Isobelle started to shake with anger; she started to pull her hair in frustration, pacing up and down.

"No, no, no," she kept repeating and then she just stopped.

Autum saw the change in her: the way she looked, her posture – it was like someone else had taken over her body. Isobelle began to shake the scaffolding above them until metal started to drop.

"Isobelle, don't! You're going to kill us both!" But Autum realised she was too far gone to care.

Autum caught sight of something out of the corner of her eye and moved her head. "Frank!" she shouted out before she could stop herself, as he tried to signal for her to shush.

"You don't think I'm going to fall for that line do you? I killed your precious, *weak* husband. He couldn't even defend his pathetic wife and his body is over there…" She turned to point to where she'd left him but there was only the plastic sheeting on the floor.

"What the…?" Before she could blink, Frank had charged her. They rolled around on the floor as Autum screamed. Isobelle bit his ear and Frank let out a screech. He knew he was dealing with no ordinary woman and reminded himself of that as she kicked him in the balls. All rational behaviour went out of the window. Autum had now joined in. Elbows flew, nails dug into flesh and blood spattered the floor. They heard a creaking noise above them and they all looked up simultaneously.

"Get out of the way!" Frank shouted to Autum as she went into a roll to dodge the scaffolding that was heading straight for them. Frank rolled too, taking Isobelle with him, despite her madness she was still pregnant with child, what they didn't realise was that they had rolled too far and fell over the wall. The next few seconds were filled with the clattering of metal, wood, dust and sheeting flying all over the place. Then silence.

Autum floated away in her mind. She felt at peace. She knew she had not survived what had happened to her but hoped that Frank had. She was surrounded by her favourite flowers, long-stemmed, white lilies. She could smell them, as fresh as day. She raised her hand in front of her and saw how pale it looked. She ran her other hand over it and she felt how smooth it was. Yes, I'm dead, she thought to herself again. She sat up and looked around her surroundings. *Where am I? Is this what it feels like to be dead?* She lay back down and waited for whatever was going to claim her.

"Goodbye, Frank," she whispered, as she closed her eyes and waited. She felt her body rocking from side to side. *This is it.* She refused to open her eyes to what awaited her but the rocking continued. She was panicking now but decided that you could not change your fate: she would be as brave and calm as she could. Light after bright light greeted her eyes, like she had been abducted by aliens. She lifted a hand to shield her eyes and heard a voice.

"She's awake."

Isobelle came around the same time that Frank did, he had tried to protect her even after all the things she had done to him, she realised that he couldn't hurt her, and his first instinct was to protect, she turned her head towards him and even wiped some dust from his face.

"He let out a cough"

"All I wanted was a baby Frank" she said on a whisper, she looked down and saw a spike jutting out of her side and put her hand on it. Blood soaked her hand and she gave a low plea for help.

"Help me Frank" as she lifted up her blood covered hand to show him.

Frank slowly lifted himself up as more rubble started to fall around them as Isobelle screamed a muffled sound.

He was in pain himself but needed them to move clear of where they were. He looked for Autum and called out her name, but he couldn't see her, he called out her name again and still no answer. As the pain ripped through his body he managed to drag Isobelle away from danger and into open space, Frank knew it looked bad but yet he kept her spirts up by mocking her attempts to kill him.

"I thought I did it out of anger, I wanted revenge, but now I want you to know the truth, that I did it because I was jealous, that you and Autum still had it all, you both left me with nothing" as she starts to cough up blood.

"Don't try and talk" Frank replied "I never realise how much you were hurting, I don't understand why you just didn't try and move on, get some help, be happy, not waste your time on revenge, look where we have all ended up once more" again he calls out for Autum.

"Promise me something, as she lifts her hand and strokes his cheek, promise me that you will give me a good send off, I know I don't deserve it…" as a tear slips down her cheek.

"I promise, but it won't come to that" Frank saw the amout of blood she was losing and knew she needed help fast.

"I hope she's ok, she's a fighter" Isobelle said.

"Just like you, now save your breath" he tried to stem the flow of blood but he couldn't.

"Tell her I'm sorry, I was jealous, I just wanted someone to love…" she whispered.

"Shush, you can tell her yourself when we get out of here."

Frank held onto her hand as he hear's siren's approach.

"Stay with me Isobelle, help is here" as he gently lets her go and fights through his pain to crawl to the open ledge and waved for help still not knowing where is wife was, but she was on the same floor he just couldn't see her before he passed out.

Isobelle had died not long after arriving at hospital he was told, she had lost too much blood, as the nurses fought to keep her alive.

He had promised to give her a good send off and Frank was a man of his word, he had shed a tear for different reasons because their life, after some serious councelling would finally settle down, he shed a tear for a wasted life *Isobelle's* and all the things he knew she could have accomplish if she hadn't taken this path.

Frank tried to protest at getting medical help until he knew his wife and child were OK. Yes, at the time he was bleeding and yes he was in pain. He had dislocated his shoulder, got a black eye, broken his leg and probably a rib or two but he was alive. When they fell they landed on the floor below that's all he knew and now he was stuck in a hospital bed. He tried to stay positive but it was hard when he had nearly lost her once before. He needed to see her but she was not awake and he was high on drugs.

His door opened and a doctor walked in.
"She's awake."

Frank could not get out of bed as his leg was stuck up in the air. He tried his utmost to break free.

"I need to see her," Frank said.

"All in good time," said the doctor. She knows that you are alright, she was asking for you.

Frank started to get emotional.

"…the baby?"

"They are both doing fine. She's one hell of a fighter," he replied.

And Frank knew she was…

The months flew by and, on September 10th, Autum gave birth to Alexander James Howard, weighing in at six pounds and twelve ounces. Little did she know that, in time, he would be accompanied by Caitlin, Anthony and Christopher.

The End

You can visit the author's website at:
www.susanharrisbooks.co.uk

Lightning Source UK Ltd.
Milton Keynes UK
UKOW04f1759210715

255591UK00001B/1/P